# F RT

London Calling

By Nicole Clarke

GROSSET & DUNLAP
Published by the Penguin Group
Penguin Group (USA) Inc., 375 Hudson Street,
New York, New York 10014, U.S.A.
Penguin Group (Canada), 90 Eglinton Avenue East, Suite
700, Toronto, Ontario, Canada M4P 2Y3
(a division of Pearson Penguin Canada Inc.)
Penguin Books Ltd, 80 Strand, London WC2R 0RL, England
Penguin Ireland, 25 St Stephen's Green, Dublin 2, Ireland
(a division of Penguin Books Ltd)
Penguin Group (Australia), 250 Camberwell Road,
Camberwell, Victoria 3124, Australia
(a division of Pearson Australia Group Pty Ltd)
Penguin Books India Pvt Ltd, 11 Community Centre,
Panchsheel Park, New Delhi - 110 017, India
Penguin Group (NZ), Cnr Airborne and Rosedale Roads,
Albany, Auckland 1310, New Zealand
(a division of Pearson New Zealand Ltd)
Penguin Books (South Africa) (Pty) Ltd, 24 Sturdee
Avenue, Rosebank, Johannesburg 2196, South Africa

Penguin Books Ltd, Registered Offices:
80 Strand, London WC2R 0RL, England

Insert background image courtesy of istockphoto.

Library of Congress Control Number: 2006029449

ISBN 978-0-448-44464-2   10 9 8 7 6 5 4 3 2 1

FLiRT

London Calling

By Nicole Clarke

Grosset & Dunlap

"Good morning, ladies and gentlemen. We will be preparing for our final descent into London's Heathrow Airport. Please make sure your seat backs and tray tables are in their full upright positions."

Melanie Henderson smiled and stretched languidly in her fully reclined seat. She'd never had such a pleasant wake-up call in her life. *London Heathrow*—the magical words rang in her ears, full of possibilities. She'd filled her journal last night with—count them—not one, not two, but three pages of London must-sees and to-dos, and once the plane touched down, she was going to make sure they all happened.

She leaned over Liv, who was still catching Z's in the seat next to her, and tried to get her first glimpse of England. But all she saw were banks of gray clouds and faint rivulets of drizzle running down the window. Well, Liv had warned her about the gloomy winter weather in England, so she shouldn't have been disappointed or surprised. But still, she'd hoped to at least see some sort of London landmark, like Big Ben, or Parliament, or the Thames.

"Could you give a girl some room to breathe?" Liv groaned, groggily opening her eyes.

"Sorry," Mel said, but she wasn't, really. She was too jacked-up to be sorry. "It's just that . . . we're here!"

Liv adjusted her seat so she could look out the window. "I'm trying to get excited. I am. But two weeks of socializing with Mum's friends doesn't sound that thrilling to me."

"*Au contraire*, Liv, it'll be two weeks of touring London in girl-bonding togetherness," Mel protested.

"Not likely," Liv said. "Mum e-mailed me an itinerary that would put even Ms. Bishop's masochistic *Flirt* schedule to shame."

"Somehow, I doubt that," Mel said. Josephine Bishop was the publisher, editor-in-chief, CEO, and tyrannical goddess-in-charge of *Flirt,* the fashion magazine in Manhattan where Mel, Liv, and their two friends, Alexa Veron and Kiyoko Katsuda, had been interning for the last six months. Alexa was the residing Photography intern, Kiyoko was the Entertainment intern, and Liv was the Fashion intern. Mel's specialty was Features, and she had both the pleasure and pain of working the closest with Ms. Bishop, so she knew better than anyone how demanding she was.

Of course, she also knew what Liv was up against with her parents. Mr. and Mrs. Bourne-Cecil, who owned a renowned art gallery in Paris, functioned in London's most pedigreed circles. Their comings and goings appeared regularly in *Hello* magazine, and they expected Liv to keep her own image impeccable by following all of the rules of

British social decorum to a T. They'd threatened to bring her back to London from New York on more than one occasion, and Liv tried hard—sometimes too hard—to do their bidding just to keep the peace. Still, even if Liv's mom ruled with a pristinely manicured but iron fist, Mel couldn't imagine her being worse than the dragon lady that was her boss. "No one rivals Josephine Bishop and her psychotic deadlines," Mel said, trying to bolster Liv's confidence and stir up at least *some* enthusiasm.

But Liv wasn't convinced. "I'll be lucky if I have time to use the loo in between all the high teas and dinner parties."

"Hey, if the Queen Mother can be overruled, so can your mom," Mel said. "We'll have plenty of time free from the parentals. You'll see."

"Ever the sunshine-and-roses girl, aren't you? But remember, you haven't met Mum yet," Liv said, ribbing her friend. She could've fooled anyone into thinking she'd just stepped out of a salon, but she still pulled out her makeup bag and patted her blond bob into place, then applied some bronzing blush, a few swipes of mascara, and peach lip gloss. It never ceased to amaze Mel how Liv could look so

"I'll be lucky if I have time to use the loo in between all the high teas and dinner parties."

fresh-faced and bright, even after an international flight that had left most of the other passengers wrinkled and zombified. The term "red-eye" simply didn't apply to her.

It was impossible for Mel to replicate Liv's makeover, but she was comfier with a no muss, no fuss routine, anyway. Since au naturel was her MO, she hurriedly swept her own hair into a loose topknot to compensate for the bedhead, rubbed the sleep out of her eyes, and settled for that. "I've never slept so great on a plane before," she said. "And now I'm convinced. The only way to survive a red-eye is to fly in style, first class all the way. Have I said thank you yet for the first-class ticket?"

"Only about a million times." Liv smiled. "It's nothing, really. My parents have loads of frequent flyer miles from their trips to the gallery in Paris. They couldn't use them all if they traveled once a week for the rest of their lives."

"I just wish Keeks and Alexa could've come, too," Mel said. "But then again, they jetted off to the land of wine and cheese in Paris without us two months ago, so I guess that makes us even."

"No doubt," Liv said. "We suffered through school while they hit the runways in Paris. So now it's their turn to hit the books while we join the jet-set crowd."

Mel grinned. "I'm just lucky my teachers let me take my midterms early. Otherwise, my parents never would've agreed to let me come with you." She and Liv had both finished up their midterms at school last week so that they'd be study-free in England. It had taken a few phone calls from their parents, but their teachers had finally relented when Mel and Liv had sold them on the great benefits of travel as a form of worldly education. And Mel had taken off from her waitressing job at Moe's until after New Year's, so both girls were work-free *and* study-free. "I'm so ready for some R & R. I'm not going to miss school, or Ms. Bishop's editorial totalitarianism, but I am going to miss our fellow Flirtistas."

Last night, she and Liv had said good-bye to Kiyoko and Alexa at their SoHo loft, also known as the Flirt-cave, while Emma Lyric, their very cool, very beatnik housemother, called for a car to take them to LaGuardia Airport for their flight to London. Even though the girls were only going to be separated for two weeks, it felt like they were prepping for a much longer time apart. And they kind of were, because even though Mel and Liv would be back in New York for a few weeks, the girls would go their separate ways for the holidays—Mel back to her beloved NorCali, Liv to Hampstead Heath, Alexa to Argentina, and Kiyoko to Tokyo. The girls would be back in January for another semester at their internships, but even so, after a whole summer and fall together, it was hard to think about being without one another for the holidays. Even last night, Mel had already started to tear up at the idea.

"Blimey," Kiyoko had said as Mel gave a round of fierce hugs to her friends, "don't even think about letting those soggy eyes overflow. If there's one thing Kiyoko hates more than listening to yesterday's oldies, it's waterworks. Lads, we're going to see each other in two weeks. This is not Armageddon."

"Whatever, Keeks," Mel said, wiping her eyes. "You know you're going to miss us."

"Maybe a little," Kiyoko admitted grudgingly. "But only because you're leaving us alone with Gen and Charlotte."

"Hey, we put up with them for two weeks without you guys, too, remember? Although you and Gen together— that is a frightening thought," Mel said. "I wonder who will strangle whom first." Even Mel, easygoing as she was, had a hard time getting along with Genevieve Bishop, the Beauty intern at *Flirt* who, because she was Josephine Bishop's niece, acted like she was entitled to royal treatment. Gen lived in the loft, too, along with Charlotte Gabel, the Electronic Content intern. Charlotte was finally starting to become her own person after months of being Gen's mini-me, but Kiyoko still harbored some resentment that Charlotte got to work with Kiyoko's former boss. "Try not to kill each other," Mel said.

“*Lads, we're going to see each other in two weeks. This is not Armageddon.*”

"Don't worry, mate. As long as Gen stays out of my way, there might be peace in our time," Kiyoko joked. "And our two species might find a way to coexist."

"At least you have each other," Liv said, grinning at Alexa.

"Miss Chiquita Banana here?" Kiyoko said. "She'll be dragging me to every catwalk within the five boroughs without you two to distract her." She ribbed Alexa in what was meant to be a semi-playful gesture, but Mel saw a scowl flicker across Alexa's face, even though she tried to hide it behind her thick waves of hair. Kiyoko and Alexa had had a falling-out in Paris when Miko, Kiyoko's sister, had hand-picked Alexa for a modeling photo shoot, leaving Kiyoko feeling left out and just a tad jealous. Kiyoko and Alexa had made up since then, but Alexa was still a little sensitive about her modeling.

"Nobody can make you do anything you don't want to, *chica loca*," Alexa said quietly. "Especially me." Then she turned to Mel and Liv with a big grin. "*Lo siento*, I'm sorry that I won't be there with you to snap some pictures of Her Royal Highness."

"Mum doesn't do candids, anyway," Liv teased, making everyone laugh. Mrs. Bourne-Cecil had already established a reputation for herself among the four girls as being one seriously high-maintenance mom, especially since she'd tried to force Liv to go back to England over the summer.

"But I fear for Prince Harry if you ever set foot on British soil, Alexa," Mel teased.

"*Yo también.* I'd give the paparazzi an even worse reputation just to get a shot at his smile. *¡Es lo máximo!*" Alexa fell to her knees, clinging to Liv's pants. "Take me with you, *por favor*."

"Next time," Liv said. "I promise. All of you will come with me."

"And in the meantime, we'll keep Bishop in line while you're gone," Kiyoko said. "Make sure she doesn't run *Flirt* into the ground or anything."

"I'd like to see that happen." Mel laughed, knowing full well that Ms. Bishop took orders from no one. She could turn Mel into a proverbial pillar of salt with one withering glance and shred her cover copy in a matter of minutes, all the while looking impeccably groomed with her chignon, frosted pearl mani, and bloodred lipstick. But Mel knew that Ms. Bishop was also amazingly good at her job—a model of professionalism, fairness, and even—shocker— bestower of the occasional hard-won compliment.

Then Emma appeared in the loft doorway. "The car service is here," she said, and the girls said their good-byes one last time.

Now, as the plane tipped toward the runway at Heathrow, Mel already found herself wondering what Kiyoko and Alexa were up to. It was one A.M. New York–time on Saturday night, which meant Kiyoko was probably

"Welcome to the mother country."

out clubbing, and that she'd missed Emma's curfew . . . *again*. Alexa had probably fallen asleep with her clothes and makeup still on, her cheek pressed to her latest photo proofs for *Flirt* and her day planner, which had the full listing of all the go-sees she'd set up for potential modeling jobs.

"Do you think Keeks and Lexa will be okay with each other while we're gone?" Mel asked Liv.

Liv tucked her *Hello* magazine into her carry-on. "I don't know," she said. "Things have been completely awkward with them. Lexa's still pretty hurt. And you know Kiyoko . . . she'll never apologize."

Mel nodded. "Maybe spending the next two weeks together without us will be good for them."

"Let's hope so," Liv said.

The plane touched down, and the girls gathered their things.

"Welcome to the mother country," Liv said as they exited the plane.

"Bloody fabulous," Mel said, attempting to sound as British as Liv.

Liv laughed. "We *have* to work on that sorry accent."

"I've got two weeks to perfect it," Mel said. Two weeks with a new country at her fingertips and the chance to explore it with her friend sounded better than fabulous—it sounded absolutely perfect.

ⓖ   ⓖ   ⓖ   ⓖ

If perfection could be topped, it was when Mel and Liv were met in the baggage claim by Giles, the Bourne-Cecils' personal driver with the perfect Brit name, and escorted to a spotless Rolls-Royce for the ride to Liv's family estate in Hampstead Heath. Giles cracked Mel up with his "Miss Olivias" and "Miss Melanies" and his robotically stiff mannerisms and posture, but she had to admit that being chauffeured through the English countryside was something she could definitely learn to live with. Although it would've been nice if the Rolls had been an eco-friendly hybrid, but she wasn't complaining.

Once the car drove through a pair of gilded gates and onto a private topiary-lined drive, Mel couldn't have lodged a complaint even if she tried, because she was rendered completely speechless by the view of Coventry Manor unfolding out the window. The trees surrounding the property were bare, but that only made the massive stone manor all the more impressive. Ivy, turned velvety red in the late-autumn chill, climbed up around the building adding a splash of brilliant color, and a fountain that would put the Trevi to shame graced the front of the drive.

"Liv, this isn't an estate," Mel said. "It's a continent."

Liv laughed. "You should see our summer estate in Tuscany." Then she blushed. "Er, pardon. That didn't come out right."

"Hey, it's nothing to be embarrassed about. I'm just happy to live the lifestyle of the rich and famous vicariously through you." Mel shrugged. "But I hope you've got a map of this place handy. You know I'm directionally impaired."

Giles stopped the car, helped the girls out, and then carried their bags inside just as a well-groomed couple that had to be Liv's parents descended the front steps.

"Olivia, darling. Lovely to see you." Mrs. Bourne-Cecil gave Olivia some restrained Euro kisses and then settled her gaze coolly on Mel. "And this must be your little friend, Melanie. Liv, you didn't tell me how charmingly . . . bohemian she was. Is her jacket vintage Chanel? How very pastoral."

Mel double-checked to see that she was, in fact, standing on British soil not more than two feet from Liv's mom. Yup, she was definitely here in the flesh. So how had she become invisible enough to be talked *about* instead of talked *to*?

"Actually, it's vintage thrift," Mel said. "And it's very nice to meet

> **Liv, this isn't an estate. It's a continent.**

you," she added, shaking hands with both Liv's parents. "Thank you so much for having me. You have a beautiful home."

"Oh, it's a work in progress, really," Mrs. B-C said dismissively. "We've been meaning to renovate for years. It's far too drafty for my taste, but Matthew likes it."

"For its old-world charm," Mr. B-C added. "Well, you girls must be peckish, not to mention exhausted. Let's get you inside where it's warm so you can get settled."

"Of course," Mrs. B-C added. "Liv, we're having a little welcome-home soiree for you this evening, so you'll want to be rested and refreshed. And Mel, I'm sure you have lots of fun plans for London sightseeing already. Giles can drive you into the city later, if you like."

Mel froze, her mouth nearly hitting the marble stairs in shock, and then laughed, relaxing. Mrs. B-C was joking, of course. No way was she going into London alone on her first night here. Finding her way around New York had been bad enough when she'd first moved there, but navigating a foreign country solo would have been impossible.

"Mel's dining with us tonight, Mum," Liv said quickly.

> ❝Mrs. B-C was joking, of course. No way was she going into London alone on her first night here.❞

The silence only lasted a split second, but Mel could've sworn the temperature dropped at least ten degrees during Mrs. B-C's pause. Mel stared in disbelief. What was up with this woman? Did she want to file a missing persons report with the U.S. Embassy after Mel took a wrong train to Scotland or something?

Finally, Mrs. B-C said, "Of course. Melanie, you're welcome to join us. And for now, Mrs. Kent's fixed you both up some tea and scones."

"Sounds delish," Mel said as they walked inside. She breathed a sigh of relief when she made it through the doorway. This was certainly better than having to leave a trail of breadcrumbs from Hampstead Heath to downtown London in hopes of someone finding her lost self. And tea and scones sounded a lot more like the trip she'd had in mind. She smiled at Liv, hoping that after that close call, this was the start of a fab two weeks.

ⓖ   ⓖ   ⓖ   ⓖ

Two cranberry-orange scones and one estate tour later, Mel was convinced she'd willingly swap places with Liv any day. The fifty-plus rooms in the manor, each one decorated more beautifully Victorian than the last, and the estate's vast gardens, horse stables, and forests—it was all even more luxurious than she'd imagined when Liv had described it back in New York. The guest suite she was staying in was outfitted with a Jacuzzi bathtub, a bidet, a dressing room, a two-room walk-in closet, a canopy bed with a plush Waterford duvet, and a huge balcony overlooking the tea garden. After a long nap and bubble bath, Mel felt refreshed and ready to tackle the Bourne-Cecils' dinner party with finesse. Once she'd discounted half the clothes in her suitcase as wrong for an evening mixing with British high society, she finally decided to track Liv down for some advice on an ensemble.

She set out for Liv's bedroom, no small feat given that the manor was roughly the length of three football fields. She practically needed a mini Tube train running through this place just to get from room to room. Even though Liv had shown Mel where her room was, the doorways in the upstairs corridor all looked alike, and Mel found a library, sitting room, and several lavish bedrooms, but no Liv. She passed another door and heard muffled rustlings from behind it. Joy of joys, maybe she'd found the right place—finally! She swung the door in, and a startled cry followed by a deafening crash echoed through the hall.

Mel winced. That did not sound good. Almost afraid to look, she peeked around the door into a dimly lit, narrow wooden stairwell to see the housekeeper, Mrs. Kent, holding an empty silver tray and staring down at what looked like the sad, shattered remains of a full tea service. Delicate china lay in pieces all over the stairs among puddles of tea and now-soggy biscuits.

"Omigod," Mel said, half-running, half-tumbling into the stairwell to help with the mess. "I'm so, so sorry."

"Quite all right, miss," Mrs. Kent replied with a small smile, brushing at her tea-soaked skirt. "These things happen."

Mel bent to pick up some of the broken china, but Mrs. Kent stopped her, "Pardon, miss, but I'll remedy this."

"Oh no, please, I want to help," Mel started, "I—"

"What on earth?" a voice cried from above, and Mel looked up to see Mrs. Bourne-Cecil at the top of the stairs, staring down at the chaos. She was dressed for the evening in a vanilla chiffon high-collar blouse and a floor-length silk skirt in midnight blue, looking dramatically out of place in the tiny, drab stairwell. She frowned at Mel as if she were something highly distasteful that was stuck to the bottom of her Ferragamo stiletto.

Mel's face flamed. *Oh, great. Way to make a first impression.*

66 She frowned at Mel as if she were something highly distasteful that was stuck to the bottom of her Ferragamo stiletto. 99

"I'm sorry," Mel said. "I was trying to find Liv's room, and I thought this might be it."

"The old butler staircase?" Mrs. B-C said with a sigh. "I think not."

Mel remembered seeing something about butler's stairs in some gloomy British film recently—the butler and housekeepers used them so that they could remain unheard and unseen by houseguests. But Mel had no idea they were actually *still* used.

"It was my fault, madam," Mrs. Kent said to Mrs. B-C. "I should have had a better grasp on the tray."

"No! It was all me," Mel said. "I opened the door and hit the tray. If you could just show me where to find a broom, I can clean this up."

Mrs. B-C rubbed her forehead, no doubt feeling a Mel-size headache coming on. "Mrs. Kent, I'll forgo my afternoon tea, thank you," Mrs. B-C said. "Come with me, Melanie. I'll take you to Liv's room."

Mel's head sunk as she whispered one last apology to Mrs. Kent and reluctantly followed Mrs. B-C into the corridor. The walk was awkwardly silent but blessedly short, since Liv's room happened to be just down the hall from the butler's staircase. Mrs. B-C opened the door into Liv's chambers (*chambers* being the only word Mel found appropriate for the cathedral-like bedroom suite before her).

"Cheers, Mel," Liv said when they walked in. "I

knew you could find my room again!"

"Well," Mrs. B-C said, "it wasn't without a little detour, but all's well now." Liv shot Mel a questioning glance, and Mel just shook her head, hoping Liv'd get the message. She did, and thankfully let the subject drop.

"I trust you're nearly ready for this evening, Olivia dear?" Mrs. B-C asked.

"Yes, Mum," Liv said.

Mrs. B-C passed her eyes with hawklike precision over Liv's burgundy Karen Millen pencil skirt, ivory sheath, and modest pearl choker, then gave a subtle nod of approval. Yeesh—and Mel had thought Ms. Bishop was a fashion dominatrix. Mel took in Liv's outfit, too, then glanced down at her own. She'd thought her filmy black peasant top and maroon wide-legged pants tied with a velvet sash would be fine for the evening. After all, she'd just worn this outfit last week to a *Flirt* cocktail party and passed Ms. Bishop's inspection. But now, after seeing Liv, she suddenly knew that her own granola look wasn't going to fly in this Givenchy-filled world she'd stepped into.

"Melanie . . ." Mrs. B-C paused, her eyes flitting over Mel's clothes. "You really should be changing, too. It's getting late, and our guests will be arriving shortly."

"Um, actually," Mel said, "I was just coming to get Liv's advice on what to wear."

"Splendid," Mrs. Bourne-Cecil said, a small smile of relief on her face. "I'm sure Olivia can help you find something suitable for this evening. See to it that you're downstairs within the hour."

Suitable, Mel repeated in her head as Mrs. B-C turned to leave. What did she look like to Mrs. B-C right now, some sort of hand-me-down roadkill?

As soon as the door clicked shut, Mel smiled at Liv. "Do you think I can borrow something for tonight? This is one of the nicest outfits I brought. I knew I should've asked Jonah for some loans from The Closet before we left Manhattan." Jonah Jones had always been ready and willing to help Mel out of many a wardrobe crisis during her internship at *Flirt*, and The Closet held near-mythic proportions of designer clothes ready for photo shoots, whiny models in need of a quick loaner, and destitute interns who wanted to pass inspection with Jo Bishop. "Do you think we could get him to airmail us a few D&G evening gowns, before your mom bans me to the stables?"

Mel laughed, and Liv squeezed her shoulder. "No one's banning you. And I think your clothes are stellar."

"Stellar they may be, but Coventry Manor they're not." Mel smiled. "I'm willing to put my fave duds aside for the evening in favor of more 'suitable' attire. So make me over, Liv. I'm fashion putty in your hands."

Twenty minutes later, Mel was dressed in a respectable Paul Smith blouse and skirt with a pair of Liv's handmade teardrop earrings as an accent.

"And voilà," Mel said, vamping in front of the

> **Coventry Manor they're not. I'm willing to put my fave duds aside for the evening in favor of more 'suitable' attire.**

mirror. "From faux pas to fab in under half an hour. Do you think I'll pass Bourne-Cecil inspection now?"

"No doubt," Liv said, smiling in approval. "But Mel, do you still feel . . . you know, like you're Melanie?"

"Hey," Mel said, "even an extreme makeover can't mess with the granola within. Right?"

Liv laughed. "Quite right."

"Now." Mel smiled. "Let's go face your adoring fans."

⟡ ⟡ ⟡ ⟡

Mel and Liv stepped into a drawing room full of Mrs. B-C's hand-selected entourage of intellectual art-critic friends, meticulously polished and sipping Framboise out of crystal aperitif glasses, and it took less than five seconds for Mel to realize that the yawn potential for this party was dangerously high. She didn't see anyone in the room under the age of forty, and the smatterings of conversations about post-modernism, narratology, and

> ## *It took less than five seconds for Mel to realize that the yawn potential for this party was dangerously high.*

white space she heard as she and Liv made their way to the bar for sodas were enough to strike a fear of boredom deep in her heart.

"I don't know how you do it," she whispered to Liv after twenty minutes of schmoozing with art gurus. "You listen to these people talk like they're the most fascinating conversationalists in the world."

Liv shrugged. "They're Mum's patrons. Some of them have known me since I was a baby. It's not so bad, really."

"You're so right. It just went from bad to fantastic," Mel said, suddenly grinning as her hottie radar picked up a signal from the far corner of the room. "I think I've just spotted our entertainment for the evening. *Who* is that?" She nodded toward said hottie, who was dressed neo-preppy in a slate turtleneck and charcoal sport coat that set off his golden curls and ice blue eyes, and was flashing a smile worth more than the authentic Renoir hanging over the marble mantelpiece.

Liv followed Mel's glance, then grinned. "That's Pierce Northam, Lord Northam's son. He's an ace bloke. He goes to Ludgrove School now, but we used to play together when we were little. We still see each other every now and again whenever our parents get together. It's totally platonic, of course. You know I go for the creative, starving-artist type over British heirs any day."

"I don't know if it's a type you go for, as much as it's one starving artist named Eli in particular," Mel teased. Eli was a film student at NYU and Liv's boyfriend of almost six months. And even though Mrs. Bourne-Cecil was in blatant denial of Liv and Eli's like-like status, Liv seemed to be falling harder for him now than ever before.

Liv blushed at the mention of Eli's name, then nudged Mel. "Well, I'm spoken for, but you're not. And that's a good thing, because Pierce has been looking you over for the last two minutes," Liv whispered. "I can introduce you, if you want. But I wasn't sure, what with Nick and everything . . ."

Nick Lyric's face flashed in front of Mel's eyes. He was their housemother's son—an enigmatic painter in New York who Mel had had an on-again-off-again flirtation with. They were good friends who'd shared one *great* kiss, but the status of their relationship was a constant looming question mark. Mel shrugged. "You know the timing's never right with me and Nick. I mean, he finally admits he has feelings for me and then—boom—he's off to Italy. But in the meantime . . ." She smiled. "What's the harm in a little foreign fling?"

"Brill. Come on then, I'll introduce you," Liv said.

She started toward Pierce, only to find that Mrs. B-C had already swooped down on the poor, unsuspecting soul and was leading him in their direction.

"Olivia," Mrs. B-C crooned, "I thought you and Pierce might want to catch up. It's been ages since you last saw each other, but you two will be dining next to each other this evening, so you'll have all night to visit." She winked at them while Mel stared in disbelief. The woman was as unstoppable as a bad hair day—no matter how hard you tried, there was no escape.

"Lovely to see you again, Liv," Pierce said. "I hear you're making waves in the fashion world now. Your mother's just been telling me all about your wonderful accomplishments at *Flirt*."

"Has she?" Liv said, smiling politely while at the same time shooting her mother a subtle but pointed I-know-what-you're-up-to look.

Pierce's eyes shifted from Liv to Mel, and then to Mrs. B-C, and Mel guessed he was waiting for Mrs. B-C to make a second introduction. But Mrs. B-C was busy beaming at Liv and Pierce, no doubt envisioning them hand in hand, the epitome of an adoring couple, gracing the cover of *Hello* magazine.

Mel was grateful when Liv took matters into her own hands. "Pierce, I'd like you to meet my friend Melanie."

"Oh, where are my manners?" Mrs. B-C cried, although she didn't look the least bit fazed. "How awful of me to forget. Yes, Melanie is one of Liv's fellow interns at *Flirt* in New York. She wants to be a writer someday. And, no doubt, she's getting some impressive tutelage from Josephine Bishop in that department."

It was only by sheer force of will and some therapeutic deep-breathing techniques that Mel managed to quash the fury rising up inside her. *Wants* to be a writer? She *was* already a writer in her own right. She did more than scribble in her journal—she'd written at least half a dozen features that met with Ms. Bishop's approval. What did Liv's mom think, that Ms. Bishop rewrote every piece of copy Mel turned in? Mel was about to launch a defense, but then was blinded by another one of Pierce's smiles, which made her suddenly forget her agenda.

"Writing," he said. "That's great. What type of pieces?"

But before Mel could answer, Mrs. B-C interjected.

"Speaking of writing," she said, taking Mel by the arm. "Melanie, Lady Ashford is compiling memoirs on her years of leading research in biology for the Royal Society. I thought you might enjoy talking to a veteran author. It's always best to garner advice from those greats who've gone before you." She beamed at Pierce and Liv as she deftly steered Mel away. "I'm sure you two have lots to chat about, so we'll leave you to it."

After one pleading glance back at Liv, Mel was ushered over to an ancient woman seated primly on the edge of a Chippendale sofa, introduced to her, and then promptly abandoned by Mrs. B-C. Over the next painful hour, Mel tried to listen politely as Lady Ashford launched into what seemed like—*yawn*—the entire history of the known universe. She barely spoke above a whisper, and stopped mid-sentence a few times to nod off. And Mel couldn't blame her. She had to catch her own eyes from drooping more than once, too. By the time dinner was announced, Mel was in a complete fugue state. Between her jet lag and hunger and the world's longest monologue, she'd hit the wall—big time. As the guests entered the dining room, with its wall-to-ceiling frescoes and magnificent chandelier, Mel excused herself from Lady Ashford and looked for Liv.

There she was on the other side of the long table, smiling demurely as Pierce pulled out her chair for her. But Mel could read a strain on Liv's face, and could practically hear her chanting a mantra in her head: *Eli, Eli, Eli.* Poor Liv. Maybe Mel could find a way to give Liv a break from Mrs. B-C's obvious matchmaking ploy . . . if she could just make her way to the seat on the other side of Pierce. But when she checked the place cards, she found that Mrs. B-C

> *Mel tried to listen politely as Lady Ashford launched into what seemed like the entire history of the known universe.*

had seated her on the other side of the table, a very safe distance from Liv and Pierce. And with growing horror, Mel suddenly realized that Liv wasn't the one who was going to need rescuing after all. Because on either side of her empty chair were—*thank you, Mrs. B-C*—Lord and Lady Ashford, smiling expectantly up at her.

She'd been banned to the geriatric ward for the evening! *Awesome.*

ⓖ ⓖ ⓖ ⓖ

Ten minutes into Lady Ashford's vivid description of her husband's gout, Mel was trying some visualization tactics to distract herself. Waterfalls, flowers—anything had to be better than the picture she had in her mind of Lord Ashford at the moment. Ever since they'd sat down, Lady Ashford had been jabbering nonstop. And it was no wonder, because Lord Ashford was so hard of hearing, he was barely aware she was speaking. So Mel guessed Lady Ashford must have been delighted to have a live, responsive audience. Mel soon became an expert at giving the obligatory nods, smiles, and verbal cues to Lady Ashford, and when the waterfall visualizations stopped working, she picked right up with daydreaming about sneaking away to her room to write in her journal.

It was only when the first plates of food finally arrived that Mel's hunger snapped her to attention.

But her hopes for the feast died when a member of the waitstaff set a gold-plated hors d'oeuvres dish in front of her, and she found herself staring at a cracker dolloped with chopped eggs, a dab of sour cream, and what looked like—überyuck—caviar.

"*Bon appetit*," Mrs. B-C said, nodding to her guests to begin devouring the sad-looking little fish-to-be's. Mel stared at her plate for a second and then decided the best course of action was to quietly abstain and hope no one noticed.

"Melanie, dear, is the caviar not to your liking?" Mrs. B-C asked, and everyone at the table grew disconcertingly quiet.

Mel cringed inwardly. So much for no one noticing.

"Not at all," she said. "It's just that I'm a vegetarian, and I recently became involved in PETA's fish empathy movement. I'll wait for the next course . . . no problem." Mel met Liv's eyes across the table and sent a reassuring smile her way, but Liv looked panic-stricken.

"Pardon, Mum," she said quietly to Mrs. B-C. "But didn't I tell you that Mel was a vegetarian earlier?"

"It's fine, really," Mel said. Then, feeling ever resourceful, she turned to Lord Ashford. "Would you like my appetizer?" she asked loudly into his hearing aid.

"Certainly, dear," he answered, taking Mel's plate from the server. "And do tell us more about this fish enema movement, if you please."

A few muffled gasps—and was there a half giggle, half snort from Pierce's general direction, too?—fluttered around the room, but Mel made sure to keep her eyes steadily focused on the tablecloth.

Nothing like a little social suicide before dinner to make a girl lose her appetite.

Somehow she managed to survive the rest of the meal without creating any more controversy, mostly by keeping her mouth shut and concentrating on what she *could* eat from her main dish, which wasn't much. Her stomach was still rumbling after she finished her asparagus and roasted potatoes, but happily, Pierce was eating veggie, too.

"We'll go meatless together," he'd said after the caviar fiasco. "I have the deepest respect for fish, too."

Mel had laughed, suddenly feeling much less like an eco-freak in the room full of pheasant-devouring Brits, and she'd somehow managed to gather up the last of her reserves to make it through the rest of dinner.

But once the guests retreated to the drawing room for port and tea, she was crashing big-time. She'd had enough of the pointless niceties and was ready to give her social-pariah self wallflower status. Thankfully, though, Liv had saved her a seat on the settee, which she practically jumped into for fear of it being snagged by someone else.

"Oh, Mel," Liv said. "This whole evening has been just awful for you. I'm so, so sorry."

"Would you quit with the apologies already?" Mel said as she collapsed next to Liv. "It's my fault I didn't make a better impression."

"What are you talking about? You made a brilliant impression." Liv giggled. "Lord and Lady Ashford will *never* forget you or your fish enema now."

"Where's your Prince Charming?" Mel teased. "I figured your mom would be announcing your illustrious engagement by now."

"Cheeky," Liv said, frowning. "He's gone to fetch me some tea and Tylenol. Thanks to Mum, I have a horrid headache. And he's *not* my Prince Charming. I don't know what Mum fancies she's up to. She likes him because he's the heir to Lord Northam's fortune and would make a 'fine catch,' as she says. But she knows I'm seriously dating Eli. Do you know what she told me earlier? 'Olivia, dear, I do hope you'll give Pierce a chance. He's got impeccable breeding, and is much more equally matched to your background and standing than that Elvin fellow.' Elvin, she called him. She doesn't even know Eli's name!"

"You and I both know Eli's perfect, and any other boy-types pale by comparison," Mel said. "It doesn't matter what everyone else thinks."

"It does when you're a Bourne-Cecil." Liv sighed. "Blimey, how you sneeze matters when you're a Bourne-Cecil."

"Tea, ladies?" a voice said, and Mel looked up at

Pierce's dazzling smile.

"Thanks," Mel said, taking a cup and sliding over on the settee to make room for him.

As Liv gratefully took her Tylenol, Pierce leaned conspiratorially towards Mel. "What you did at dinner tonight? That was brill."

Mel laughed. The fact that Pierce wasn't offended automatically knocked her opinion of him up a few notches. "Well, I don't do fish *or* fish eggs."

"But to turn down *Almas* caviar?" Pierce said, nodding in admiration. "That qualifies as a coupe."

Mel gave Liv a questioning look, and Liv said, "Almas is *the* best caviar, Mel."

"What, in England?" she asked.

"In the world," Pierce said.

"It costs about fourteen thousand quid per tin," Liv whispered.

Mel quickly did the math in her head, then gasped. "But that's twenty-five grand!" She put her head in her hands. "Omigod. I can't believe that people actually eat tiny eggs that cost more than my parents' car. And I can't believe I refused to eat it."

Pierce grinned. "I say cheers to that. I've never met anyone with the guts to turn it down until tonight."

"Thanks, I think," Mel said, blushing under Pierce's gaze. Was she wrong, or was there a hint of flirting in the way he was looking at her? She smiled. "Glad to know I've

> **I never knew being a British deb was such hard work.**

found an ally."

And she had, because over the next half hour, she and Pierce talked about everything from global warming to animal rights. Liv had been whisked away by her parents to say good-bye to departing guests, and Mel was more than happy to talk to Pierce in the meantime. He was funny, smart, drop-dead gorge, and—*huge* plus—a greenie-sympathizer. By the time Lord Northam had called for his car and Pierce stood up to leave, Mel was sad to see him go.

"Well, Mel," Pierce said, "I hope we'll be seeing more of each other while you're here."

Mel's heart tap-danced across her chest. "I hope so, too." Then, seeing the scathing glance Mrs. B-C was giving her from the doorway, Mel added, "I mean, I'm sure Liv will be seeing you, and, um . . . I guess I'll see you then, too." She cringed. What kind of speech impediment was she suffering from now? One obviously brought on by a bad case of Mrs. Bourne-Cecil, who was rapidly walking toward them.

"Pierce, do tell me what your plans are while you're home," Mrs. B-C said, leading him into the entryway. "I'm sure Liv would *love* to get better acquainted with you again, and I have her schedule right here . . ."

Mel sighed and flopped back onto the couch, where Liv found her a few minutes later.

"I never knew being a British deb was such hard work," Mel said. "How do you do it?"

Liv managed a weary smile. "Sadly, it's been bred into me. There's no escape. So . . . bedtime?"

"You're not kidding," Mel said, hoisting herself off the couch, then pulling Liv to her feet. "And maybe tomorrow we can hit the town? I feel London calling."

"Tomorrow." Liv grinned. "I promise."

Once Mel was settled into her layers of silky soft sheets, she pulled out her journal. It had been a whirlwind first day, and before she succumbed to the jet-lag-induced sleep of the dead, she wanted to get what she could down on paper:

From the Journal of Melanie Henderson
Saturday, November 25

Fact: After tonight, it's completely confirmed. In the eyes of Liv's family, I am a total plebe and heir-nabber. Mrs. B-C doesn't think I'm fit to kiss her perfectly pedi'd feet.

Fact: There are fifty people in Britain tonight digesting a hundred thousand dollars' worth of fish eggs. Don't the ridiculously wealthy have better uses for their money? Like saving the endangered beluga sturgeon instead of eating its potential offspring? A thought to ponder.

Fact: Pierce Northam is the gorgeous heir to a small British empire and Liv's intended (hand-picked by Mrs. B-C), but could he also be a friend to fishes everywhere (and possibly a hippie-yank named Melanie)? Must explore this possibility by staring deeply into Pierce's eyes (yummola) to gather further information. It's almost enough to make me forget I won't be seeing Nick for two years.

Fact: Out of the sixteen hours I've been in England, I've spent four sleeping, zero sightseeing (not to mention shopping), eight schmoozing with stuffy old Brits, one in post-hottie glow mode thinking about Pierce, and three yakking with Liv. Tomorrow, will make sure that yakking and sightseeing with Liv take top priority.

Fact: I am on international soil for the first time in my life. How cool is that? And no matter how difficult Liv's parentals make it, Liv and I are going to have the time of our lives while we're here.

chapter two

Alexa checked her watch for the third time, but no matter how hard she willed it to run backward, it still read one thirty P.M. She was already thirty minutes late to fifth period bio. *Ay!* In what delusional universe had she ever thought she could make it all the way over to Chelsea and back to her school, Saint Catherine's, in under an hour?

She shoved her modeling portfolio into her bag as the cab rounded the corner to the school, and she had her door open before the car even stopped.

"Watch it, miss," the cabbie growled. "You want to hurt yourself?"

"No, *lo siento*," Alexa mumbled, tossing a ten into the front seat before jumping out. In fact, she was trying to *keep* from getting hurt—not from the cabbie's maniacal driving, but from the wrath of Mother Michael, her principal, which was far more likely to actually be fatal.

She rushed up the steps and into the school. She could still make it to the last twenty minutes of her class, if she could just get past the main office undetected. She said a quick Hail Mary—a tactic she only resorted to in moments of sheer desperation. Five steps to go and she'd be in the clear. *Four, three, two—*

"Did this woman have Alexa's bag tapped with some sort of holy listening device?"

"Miss Veron!" a voice called out, but Alexa knew from the chilling tone it wasn't the divine intervention she'd been looking for. She froze, sagging in defeat, and walked into the office to face the penetrating gaze of Mother Michael. Any way she looked at it, there was nothing scarier than an angry nun, except maybe for an angry nun who could call her parents at the drop of a hat. Now that was truly terrifying.

"Sister Hazel informed me that you failed to come to her class after lunch today," she said. "I hope your excuse is a good one." She folded her arms and waited, her face a stern mask.

"I had to leave campus at lunch to run an errand," Alexa said, "and I guess I lost track of the time."

"Can you elaborate, please?" Mother Michael tapped her fingers against her forearm, waiting.

"A *muy importante* errand?" Alexa tried again.

Mother Michael sighed. "This errand wouldn't have anything to do with modeling, would it?"

Alexa gulped. *Dios mio*, did this woman have Alexa's bag tapped with some sort of holy listening device? "I got the call for the go-see at the very last minute," Alexa explained. "It was for Chanel. I had to go, just to check it out."

"Just like you had to go to the casting call for Lancôme last week, and Dolce & Gabbana the week before?" Mother Michael said, raising her eyebrows incredulously. "I thought after your Paris trip last month, you decided modeling wasn't for you. I agreed to let you take that trip with the understanding that you'd make up all of your school work and come back fully prepared to finish the semester on a strong note. This does not bode well for you."

Alexa knew it was all true. She'd left Paris planning to devote all her time to *Flirt*, her photography, and her studies. She'd promised her parents as much, and they hadn't even tried to mask their relief when she'd told them her plan.

"*Gracias a dios,*" her *mami* had said, "All those scantily-clad *modelos* strutting on the runways. They don't know the meaning of modesty, not like you, *mija*."

Alexa'd had no idea how much her parents disliked her brief stint as a model, but she never realized how much she'd miss modeling after it was over, either. The memory of walking down the runway in Paris still thrilled her to the core. And how was she to know that Miko, Kiyoko's sister, had been talking her up as the next big cover girl to all of her Manhattan connections? She'd only been back in New York for a week when calls started coming in from casting agents and, even better, designers themselves. Alexa had turned down half a dozen audition invites before the temptation got to be too much. She'd finally caved, and now she had five go-sees on her calendar between now and next week. Photography was her first love, and always would be, but why couldn't modeling be her second? And school . . . well, school could be worked in there . . . somewhere. At least, that was what she had to convince Mother Michael of right now.

"I'll try harder," Alexa said, hoping these were the magic words Mother Michael wanted to hear.

Mother Michael studied Alexa's face long and hard, then finally said, "See that you do. Your midterms start next Monday, and I hope you start focusing more on them and less on your 'extracurricular' activities. I don't want to have to call your parents about this."

Alexa swallowed down her racing heart and turned toward her bio class. "*Gracias*, Mother Michael. I'll do my best. *Yo prometo*. I promise."

> **"And school . . . well, school could be worked in there . . . somewhere."**

She was halfway down the hallway already when Mother Michael called out, "Oh, and Miss Veron? You might want to change before going to class. You know how Sister Hazel feels about dress code violations, and I'd rather not see you back in my office *again* today."

Alexa stopped and glanced down at her Seven jeans and curve-hugging sweater. Oops. She'd forgotten to change back into her Saint Catherine's uniform after the go-see. She shrugged and risked a little laugh, then rushed into the bathroom to throw on her school clothes as relief flooded over her.

She could do it all, couldn't she? Now all she had to do was make sure her grades didn't suffer, or her parents and Mother Michael would put the kibosh on her go-sees from now until the end of time.

ⓖ   ⓖ   ⓖ   ⓖ

By three thirty that afternoon, Mother Michael's lecture had become a dim memory in the face of Alexa's fave double espresso mocha and an hour in the photo lab at *Flirt*'s midtown offices in the Hudson-Bennett building. She took another sip of her elixir of choice and looked one more time at her photo prints under the light box. She had five she was happy with, out of the fifty she'd taken over the last week. Now all she had to do was add them to her portfolio. She didn't even hear the door to the lab open, and it was only a tap on her shoulder that startled her out of her deep concentration.

"Kiyoko!" Alexa gasped, nearly dumping the rest of

her mocha all over her proofs, but recovering just in time. "You scared me, *chiquita*."

"Sorry, lad." Kiyoko grinned, waving a pair of tickets in front of Alexa's face. "But I come bearing gifts, and also to save you from impending extinction. Our favorite neighborhood fuehrer has been waiting for you in the conference room for the last ten minutes, and her nostrils are starting to flare. Did you forget our staff meeting? You know, the one we go to every Monday, where we minions give the obligatory 'Yes, my liege'-ing to Ms. Bishop?"

"*Ay,* no! I forgot." Alexa groaned. "Is Lynn in there already?" Her direct supervisor, Lynn Stein, would be very unhappy that Alexa was holding up a meeting with Ms. Bishop, who was a serious stickler for punctuality.

"Lynn, Trey, Belle, everyone except *vu et moi,*" Kiyoko said. "I was sent on reconnaissance."

Alexa hurriedly turned off the light box and grabbed her prints, which slipped out of her hands and onto the floor.

"What are you working on, anyway?" Kiyoko asked, bending down to examine the prints. "Hey, these are some great pics of you! Who took them?"

"I did," Alexa said hesitantly. "I've been working on some self portraits in the studio after hours." She paused, making a split-second decision about whether she should spill everything to Kiyoko or not. "I'm adding them to my modeling portfolio," she finished, and then waited anxiously for Kiyoko's response.

"*Tutus and men in tights are so not my thing, but I'm just a pawn here.*"

Ever since they'd gotten back from Paris, Alexa had been careful not to mention modeling too much in front of her. She didn't want to rub it in Kiyoko's face that she'd been offered a modeling contract, and she had the sneaking suspicion that Kiyoko had been relieved when Alexa had decided to focus on photography instead. But now that Alexa was feeling the itch to get back into modeling, how would Kiyoko handle it? She had a short fuse, and the last thing Alexa wanted to do was set her off again, especially when Mel and Liv—the two peacemakers—were out of town.

But malleable as ever, Kiyoko surprised her now by nodding in approval. "Cool, lad," she said. "That's what I wanted to ask you about, too. Come on, let's walk while I talk. If we don't get to that meeting, Bishop will be serving our heads on a platter." As they rushed down the *Flirt* hallways, Kiyoko explained that Belle Holder, the Entertainment editor and Kiyoko's direct report, had given her two tickets to the New York City Ballet's opening night gala at Lincoln Center for their new season of interpretive dance.

"Tutus and men in tights are so not my thing," she said, "but the choreography is experimental free-form set to psychedelic trance music, and Belle wants a review for the *Flirt* website, so I'm just a pawn here. But I nabbed an extra ticket for you, because guess who designed the costumes for the season? And who's going to be putting in an appearance at the gala tonight? Hint: You saw his work during Fashion Week and have been drooling over it ever since."

Alexa stopped mid-stride. "Bjorn V?" she asked in disbelief. *"Madre del dios."*

"That's right, *mi amiga."* Kiyoko smiled. "Tonight, you can meet the man himself, face-to-face. You show him your portfolio, and who knows? Maybe you'll be his cover girl when he launches his first collection next fall."

Alexa was speechless. Bjorn V was *the* hottest— and hautest—new designer in the New York fashion scene, and to get a chance to show her portfolio to him would be a dream come true. And Kiyoko—what kind of holiday gift-giving bug had she been bitten by? Was this her way of making nice after the last month of walking on eggshells? If it was, that was fine by Alexa. In fact, that was *fantastique.*

"So are you in?" Kiyoko asked with a smile as they reached the conference room door.

"Of course, Kiyoko-*cita*!" Alexa said. "Assuming that I survive the next five minutes, that is."

But when they walked into the room, the steely silence from Lynn Stein and ice-queen glare from Ms.

Bishop made Alexa doubtful she'd survive at all. Delia, Ms. Bishop's witchy assistant, was smiling smugly, waiting for the inevitable trial by fire, which made Alexa break out in a cold sweat.

"Thank you for tracking down our lost little lamb, Miss Katsuda," Ms. Bishop said, and then turned her piercing Medusa-esque eyes to Alexa. "And Miss Veron," Ms. Bishop continued. "It would behoove you to keep in mind that lateness does not equal greatness unless you're Coco Chanel."

Alexa blushed, nodded, and quickly took her seat next to Lynn, but not before catching sight of Gen Bishop's subtle but undeniable smirk from across the table.

"Now, as I was saying," Ms. Bishop said, "we'll need to give special attention to our upcoming holiday issue. The concept will be 'Naughty and Nice'—a combining of cutting-edge couture with holiday color schemes and themes."

"Ms. Bishop," Belle said. "I'd like to suggest a divergence from the holiday themes this year. They're overdone and unoriginal. What if we satirized holiday themes and took an anti-Christmas approach? No tinsel,

> **It would behoove you to keep in mind that lateness does not equal greatness unless you're Coco Chanel.**

golds, greens, or reds. *A Christmas Carol,* Tim Burton–style—"

"Ms. Holder," Ms. Bishop interrupted. "We can't massacre the holidays. It's universal and one of our highest-selling issues annually. We'd risk losing more readers if we scrooged them out of a holiday issue. Perhaps in one of our spring issues we can try a more unconventional theme." She turned her attention to the rest of the room. "As some of you know already, the new fashion magazine *Élan* will be launching its first issue in a few weeks, and we're in danger of losing readers to our competitor unless we make a particularly strong showing with this issue. To that effect, Barney's has given us an exciting opportunity for renewed exposure. The store has invited *Flirt* to design their holiday window displays based on this issue's features." Her eyes flickered from Alexa to Kiyoko to Gen and Charlotte. "The *Flirt* interns will be in charge of putting together the displays, and the unveiling will be Saturday, December 9."

Alexa caught Kiyoko's eye and they shared an excited smile.

"I trust you won't disappoint us," Ms. Bishop addressed the four girls. "And," she added with a pointed look at Alexa, "that the displays will be ready right on time."

"Excuse me, Aunt—er, Ms. Bishop," Gen interjected. "But shouldn't Olivia and Melanie take on some of the responsibility for this project, too?"

Alexa gripped the sides of her chair in an attempt

not to roll her eyes. Leave it to brown-nosing Gen to make sure all the interns were treated equally when it came to workload.

"Gen, I appreciate your concern for the other interns," Ms. Bishop said, "but I've e-mailed them their assignments already. Melanie will be writing a feature piece on British holiday fashion, and Olivia will be creating holiday-themed jewelry for the Barney's mannequins."

Alexa watched, triumphant, as Gen turned several different shades of red and kept her head down, taking copious notes, for the rest of the meeting. Maybe it was wrong, but Gen was such a wench sometimes that Alexa couldn't help feeling at least a little sadistic pleasure from her pain.

Alexa spent the rest of the meeting half listening, half daydreaming about how she'd present her portfolio to Bjorn V tonight. When Ms. Bishop finally called the meeting to an end, Alexa practically jumped out of her seat, anxious to wrap things up for Lynn so she could get back to the loft in time to prep for the gala. Kiyoko was waiting for her at the door, and as Alexa walked out with the others, she heard Ms. Bishop ask Belle to stay behind.

"Alexa," Ms. Bishop said, "would you mind shutting the door behind you? We have some important matters to discuss."

"What was that all about?" Kiyoko asked once the four girls were out in the hallway.

"*No sé*. I don't know," Alexa said.

"I do," Gen said proudly. "Aunt Josephine told my mother all about it. She's concerned because Belle's not a good team player. Her ideas have been so over-the-top lately, like last week when she wanted to run that Entertainment feature about nude moshing on the *Flirt* website, with live concert footage. In what delusional world would she be able to pull *that* off? And she's ignored direct orders from Trey and Aunt Josephine a ton of times."

"But she's hit on some brill stories that way," Kiyoko argued. "She's an innovator, not an imitator, like some other people I could think of."

Alexa nearly snorted her last bit of coffee at that remark, but it didn't even register on Gen's face. The girl was completely oblivious.

"All I know is, if Belle doesn't take it down a notch, she's going to get herself into trouble," Gen said.

As Gen and Charlotte walked away, Alexa saw concern etched on Kiyoko's face.

"You don't think Belle's in real trouble, do you?" Kiyoko said. "If anything happened to her, what would they do with me?"

"*De nada*. It's nothing," Alexa said. "*No te preocupas.* I don't have anything to wear to the gala tonight, so forget

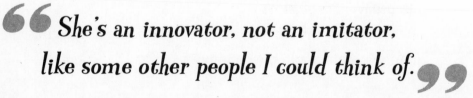

66 She's an innovator, not an imitator, like some other people I could think of. 99

about Belle for now. Let's go raid The Closet."

Kiyoko grinned, and Alexa could see the traces of worry disappearing from her face. "Belle? Who's Belle?"

ⓖ   ⓖ   ⓖ   ⓖ

They found Jonah Jones in his element, surrounded by a handful of string-bean thin models whining for clothes. But when Jonah saw Alexa and Kiyoko, he blew them kisses and clapped his hands authoritatively.

> *We come to you for help, guidance, and Gucci.*

"All right, my little waifs, you've sucked me dry," Jonah said, shooing the pouting models outside. "Now scat, before I turn you all in to Armaniholics Anonymous." He collapsed against the wall in feigned exhaustion as soon as they'd shut the door. "A fashionista's work is never done."

"Oh great guru Jonah-*san*," Kiyoko said, bowing theatrically. "We come to you for help, guidance, and Gucci." Kiyoko flashed the tickets to the Lincoln Center gala, but Jonah waved them away, staggering backward like they were poisoned.

"Oh, I can't take it," he cried. "Not another evening of those half-dead Upper-West-Siders parading around in puritanical head-to-toe draperies. I've reached my quota for galas already, and the holiday season has just started."

"*Por favor*, we're desperate," Alexa said.

"So sorry, pets, but Jonah's finito on dirge-apropos gowns. I'm starting a campaign. MADD—Mavens Against Drab Designing."

"But Jonah," Alexa pleaded, "Bjorn V's going to be there tonight. How can I show him my modeling portfolio in the guise of a lowly intern?"

"Bjorn V, you say? His premiere collection's going to be the greatest thing since stilettos. Well, that *is* special," Jonah said, tapping his finger against his chin thoughtfully.

Alexa could see he was softening, so she turned on her best pout, and he finally threw up his hands in defeat. "Oh, quit with the doe-eyes already before I start feeling like I just shot Bambi's mother. I'm yours."

"We're not worthy!" Alexa said, grinning.

"Oh stop," Jonah said, but he was obviously enjoying it. "Now, you'll need something that cries *en fête* but not funereal. Sophisticated with an air of abstract expressionism. Classy with just a drop of kitschy."

"Who says we need gowns?" Kiyoko asked, motioning to her hibiscus red micro mini. "Just give me some glass slippers to go with this, and I'm set."

Jonah gaped in horror. "Vinyl? Over my fab body! Have I taught you nothing? Am I in some nightmare version of *Pretty Woman* where Julia goes to the opera in her street clothes?" He clicked his tongue in disapproval. "No, no, we can go above-the-knee without the synthetics. Short is the new white-tie chic. You heard it here first." He snapped his fingers in triumph. "I've got just the thing for you, Alexa." He swiveled toward a rack in the back, waving them to follow.

"Those glorious curves are crying out for some pampering, so don't neglect them. If you've got it, haute it," Jonah said, tossing an aubergine Moschino dress lightly over his head for Alexa to catch as he moved on to seemingly endless shelves of shoes. "There once was a goddess who lived in a Choo," he said, flinging a pair of ooh-la-la slingbacks at Alexa. "She got so many modeling jobs, she didn't know what to do."

Alexa ran her hands over the rich purple fabric of the dress. *"Muy de la banana,"* she said.

Kiyoko eyed Alexa's outfit, then turned to Jonah. "And what am I, Cinderella's evil stepsister?"

"My, my, put those claws away, Miss Snitty Kitty," Jonah said, "and get over your Venus envy. You're next." He whisked through his clothing racks, snapping the hangers

❝Those glorious curves are crying out for some pampering, so don't neglect them. If you've got it, haute it.❞

"Prêt-à-party, darlings." with precision as he discarded one idea after another. Finally, he pulled out a Prada silk all-in-one in shimmery champagne hues. "A cat-suit for Miss Katsuda. And for an accessory . . ." He pulled out a pearl dog-collar choker.

"Snap!" Kiko said, smiling as she held the bodysuit up against her long legs.

Alexa grabbed her by the arm and pulled her into the dressing room, and two minutes later they both emerged. Alexa struck a pose in the full-length mirror and beamed. The purple in the dress brought out the olive in her skin and the auburn highlights in her thick masses of dark, curly hair, giving her an exotic bohemian air. Its fitted waist, short flare skirt, and plunging open back highlighted all of her best features. And Kiyoko looked just as amazing. The bodysuit was sleek and sophisticated, elongating her body and giving her hair a divine ebony sheen. The choker added just the right finishing touch.

"We are the bomb," Kiyoko said.

"Prêt-à-party, darlings," Jonah said, looking them over with the proud air of a creator unveiling his masterpieces. "You look positively scrumdiddlyumptious. Jonah came, Jonah saw, Jonah coutured."

Alexa and Kiyoko gave him Euro kisses as they stepped out of The Closet and made their way back to the cube farm. Alexa had just enough time to finish going through the photo proofs she'd promised Lynn before leaving to get ready for the gala. But first, she wanted to check her portfolio one more time, to make sure everything was *perfecto* for Bjorn V.

☙   ☙   ☙   ☙

"Where is he?" Alexa asked for what she knew was probably the twentieth time as she scoured the room with her camera lens. "He should be here by now. What if he's not coming?"

Next to her, Kiyoko rolled her eyes. "Blimey, you'd think this was a travesty even bigger than Kelly Clarkson going platinum. Kill the drama queen act and try to enjoy yourself, lad. Take a look around you. Have you ever had so many celebs at your camera's disposal?"

Alexa grudgingly looked around, knowing it was true. They'd only been at the post-ballet gala for ten minutes, and already she'd snapped Keira, Orlando, and Angelina. This place was a star magnet, and she had the consolation of knowing that even if—*sob!*—Bjorn V never showed up, she had enough celeb shots for *Flirt* to make Lynn happy for at least a month. And Alexa *needed* to do something to appease her after showing up late to the meeting that afternoon.

"Come on," Kiyoko said. "Let's grab some champagne to sip on and do as Manhattan's elite do—

mingle and drop six-syllable words and foreign phrases every once in awhile to sound incredibly worldly and knowledgable. I want to see if I can get some good quotes about the show to use in the review."

"Sure." Alexa shrugged, accepting defeat. But just as she'd taken her first sip of bubbly, applause started at the front of the room and spread to the back as the sea of people parted to reveal a thirty-something man in a sleek azure tux, Ferragamo boots, and a gold beret nodding graciously to his clapping and huzzahing admirers. He didn't last thirty seconds before being surrounded by nearly every single model-wannabe in the room.

"That's him," Alexa whispered gleefully, elbowing Kiyoko.

"I can see that from his harem of followers," Kiyoko said. "Word must have gotten out in the fashion circuit." Kiyoko slid Alexa's champagne out of her hand. "Go get him, tiger. You can find me later."

Alexa smiled gratefully at Kiyoko, who genuinely, and surprisingly, seemed to be rooting for her, and tucked her camera under one arm and her portfolio under the other. "Be back in a few," she called over her shoulder.

As she made her way toward Bjorn V, she tried to decide on the best tactic for an introduction. With all the Stepford wife–types surrounding him, she'd have to find a way to set herself apart. So instead of joining them right away, she stayed on the periphery, doing what she did best: photography. She snapped one candid after another, smiling in satisfaction when she saw a few of her competitors strike poses that were anything but vogue. Was that a subtle thong adjustment she's just seen? *Click!* And the slip of one girl's plunging neckline revealed some suddenly not-so-discreet tape jobs reminiscent of J.Lo. *Click*.

She didn't know how long she moved around the circle, letting her shutter do the talking. But when she finally pulled her eyes away from the lens, she saw Bjorn V watching her with avid curiosity, and then—*yes!*—motioning her over.

"And who might you be, Miss Paparazzo?" he asked.

"Alexa Veron," she replied, her heart shooting jolts of electricity to her core. She held up her *Flirt* press pass for him. "Photo intern . . . and aspiring model." There. She'd done it. She took a deep breath and waited for him to lump her in with the other girls, but instead, he held out his hand for her camera.

"May I?" he asked, and Alexa nodded, passing over her precious cargo. This was it. He was going to confiscate her memory card, or worse, her entire *Flirt*-issued camera. But instead, he hit the REVIEW button and skimmed through the pictures on the screen.

"Interesting," he muttered, laughing out loud at

some of the shots, although Alexa noticed that none of her rivals thought their bloopers-caught-on-film were even remotely funny. "And idiosyncratic. I like them. Can you show me more?" His eyes settled on the portfolio under her arm.

"*Por supuesto,*" Alexa said. "Of course." She pulled her self-portrait shots from her portfolio. "I took these myself. I think they're the most authentic in my portfolio."

"That's a strong assumption." Bjorn V flipped through the photos, pausing at one of Alexa in profile. "This isn't your best side," he said matter-of-factly, "but I think you know that already. Your left side would have made a more beautiful profile shot."

Alexa nodded, thrilled that he got that about her. "My right's not my best side, but it's my most interesting."

Bjorn V looked at her quizzically, and then a smile crept across his face. "Let's sit down, shall we?" he said, leading her to one of the settees in a quiet corner as the rest of his harem slowly drifted away. "I'd like to see your portfolio . . . all of it."

After that, everyone else in the room dropped from view. There was only Alexa and Bjorn, talking and reviewing her pictures. She talked to him about her love of photography and her photo shoot in Paris, and he described his vision for his first collection.

"I don't want cookie-cutter pretty faces," he said.

"I want personality . . . vitality." He handed her back her photos, along with his card. "I'm doing a photo shoot this Friday at eleven A.M. at Rockefeller Center, and I'd like you to come for an audition. We'll meet at the Rock Center Christmas tree. Can you make it?"

Alexa nearly jumped off her seat with excitement, but caught herself just in time. *"Sí, sí,"* she said breathlessly. "I'll be there."

They said good night, and Alexa practically floated as she gathered her things to go find Kiyoko. She couldn't wait to tell her the news. The most coveted designer on the rise, and he'd personally asked her to audition for him. This was huge! She hoped Kiyoko would be happy for her. But wait—where *was* Kiyoko, anyway?

Suddenly, the vast emptiness of the room dawned on her. The only people still remaining were the waitstaff, who were clearing away empty wine glasses and tossing half-eaten hors d'oeuvres. With growing panic, Alexa checked her watch. *Ay, ay, ay!* It was after midnight! She'd been talking to Bjorn V for over two hours. No doubt, Kiyoko'd given up on her and headed back to the loft already, and who could blame her? Alexa would have done the same thing if *she'd* been ditched. Oh, this was *muy, muy mal.* She'd missed curfew and abandoned

❝ I don't want cookie-cutter pretty faces, I want personality . . . vitality. ❞

Kiyoko, who'd gone out of her way to score Alexa a ticket for tonight in the first place!

She grabbed her coat and headed outside to hail a cab downtown. There was no way she could make it past Emma tonight without fessing up to what had happened. And Kiyoko. Well, even if Kiyoko was still speaking to her (which wasn't too likely, at least not at this time of night), Alexa was going to have a lot of explaining, and even more apologizing, to do.

chapter three

Well, it's official," Liv said Monday night, dumping her shopping bags on the floor and collapsing onto her bed, where Mel was stretched out, tapping away on her *Flirt* laptop. "Too much fake smiling is hazardous to your health. Tell me, are my cheeks black and blue?"

Mel glanced up from her typing. "Nope, but, um, don't take this the wrong way or anything . . . why is your face twitching?"

"Two words: Lady Berkshire," Liv said in a voice tinged with exhaustion. "I had a perma-grin glued to my face all through high tea with her and her two horrid daughters, and through Mum's luncheon at the National Portrait Gallery. I think I may have done long-term damage. Whoever said beauty is suffering didn't know the half of it." She'd worn her best Princess Di "I'm so divinely happy even though I'm secretly miserable" face all day, and now her cheeks, her lips, and yes, even her *teeth* physically hurt.

Mel shrugged. "But it looks like your pain paid off already." She pointed to Liv's Vivienne Westwood garment bag draped across the foot of the bed.

" *Well, it's official. Too much fake smiling is hazardous to your health.* "

"Yes, well, Mum wanted me to have a new gown to wear to next Friday's ball at the Tate for Maia Cardinale," Liv said.

Mel slapped her forehead theatrically. "A ball gown! What a loser I am. I *knew* I was forgetting to pack something. I must have left mine at home, you know, right next to my Cartier jewels."

Liv laughed, sliding out of her Burberry kitten heels with a relieved sigh. "We'll find you something to wear. Don't worry. But after the day I've had, I'm in serious need of a long soak and some trashy telly."

"Hey, at least you spent your day chatting it up with Britain's crème de la crème. You could have spent the last two days palling around with London's best big red bus drivers." Mel was smiling as she said it, but Liv detected the tiniest bit of hurt in her voice, too. "I knew I'd sunk to new social lows when one Jimmy Clarke, of Bus #300, invited me to dinner with his wife and kids. He actually looked disappointed when I told him I had to get started on my 'Brit Fashion UnThamed' feature instead."

"Mel, I'm sorry," Liv backpedaled, guilt flushing her

A ball gown! I knew I was forgetting to pack something. I must have left mine at home, you know, right next to my Cartier jewels.

face. "I've been so busy whining about my day, I forgot to ask about yours."

Mel shrugged. "I saw the winter exhibit at Kew Gardens this morning, and then checked out Harvey Nichols and a few other stores near Sloane Street for the *Flirt* feature. Then finished up with a ginger beer at a pub in Piccadilly."

"So you saw a lot. That's terrif!" Liv said, but when Mel didn't match her enthusiasm, she paused. "I know it's been a bit rough for you, touring on your own today. But Mum's had me so bloody busy . . ." She sighed. What was she, twelve? She sounded completely daft. She was supposed to be hanging with Mel, one of her closest friends, not keeping up appearances for her mum's sake. Why couldn't she just put her foot down about that, for once?

"Hey, no prob," Mel said. "Really. I'm having a great time."

Liv could see Mel was trying her best to make a good show of it in her optimistic way, but Liv wasn't buying. "I've just hit on a brilliant idea," she said. "Tomorrow's amazingly free, so why don't we go to Stratford-upon-Avon? Sans Mum, Lady Berkshire, and Jimmy Clarke. William Shakespeare's birthplace is bound to be a great source of literary inspiration for you."

"That was on my list of must-sees!" Mel said, her face lighting up.

"I could check with Mum to see if Giles can drive us." She paused. "Although she probably won't be too keen on losing him for the full day."

"In that case, here's a brainstorm: We could take a slightly more barbaric form of transport," Mel said with a grin. "The train!"

Liv laughed. "Right. So we're all set, then. You'll love it, Mel. It's such a quaint little town, and it's full of antique bookstores, and—"

Just then there was a knock on the bedroom door, and her mum stuck her head around.

"Olivia, dear," she said. "I forgot to mention earlier that we've been invited to join Lord Northam for his annual fox hunt tomorrow. He told me Pierce is especially looking forward to seeing you there." Her coy smile practically spelled out L-O-V-E, and Liv cringed. "We'll be leaving promptly at nine. And Melanie, you can attend, of course, as well. I assume you ride English?"

"Um, not exactly," Mel said.

"Actually, Mum," Liv started, "Mel and I were just chatting about tomorrow, and . . ." she faltered. *Just spit it out,* she told herself. *You can do this. Don't be such a ninny.* But it was hopeless. ". . . and we'll be there," she finished, defeated again.

"We'll be there?!" Mel cried as soon as the door was safely shut. "Nuh-uh. Not a chance. Liv, I don't ride English, whatever that means. I don't ride at all! I don't

" I assume you ride English? " trust any animal that's bigger than I am, either. And fox *hunting*?" She whispered the word like it was far too abhorrent to say out loud. She held her stomach. "Oh, I can't even think about it without feeling nauseated. No, you are definitely going solo on this one, my friend. I'm going to Stratford-upon-Avon instead, where I won't have to witness any traumatic killings."

"But, Mel, you have to come with me," Liv pleaded, panic rising in her throat. "I can't spend the whole day alone with Pierce. It'll give everyone the wrong impression. Besides, there's no killing. Since the ban on fox hunting two years ago, Lord Northam does trail-hunting instead. The dogs follow a fake fox scent. It's just to keep up the tradition, really, that's it."

Mel stared at Liv's comforter, considering. "I don't know . . ."

"Please," Liv said. "We'd get to spend the day together, and . . ." She elbowed Mel playfully. "You'd get to see Pierce again. Which, I think, wouldn't put you out *too* much, would it?"

Mel gave Liv a warning look, and then giggled. "You might actually be a scarier matchmaker than your mom."

"It's the act of a desperate woman," Liv said. "So?"

"So," Mel said. "I think I'm going to need a crash course in horseback riding."

⊙ ⊙ ⊙ ⊙

By ten A.M. Tuesday morning, it was obvious to Liv that Mel was going to need way more than a crash course. She was going to need a crash helmet, preferably of the very big, impenetrable steel variety. After five failed attempts to help Mel mount Ellison, the calmer and gentler of Liv's two horses, Liv was having serious doubts about Mel's ability to make it through the hunt without breaking her neck. She and Pierce had already spent the better part of an hour trying to teach Mel some riding basics, and Liv was hoping that some of it—at least the "how to stop the horse" part—had sunk in with Mel, but it wasn't looking too promising.

The rest of the hunt guests, including her mum and dad, were already mounted and positioned behind the Master and the other head riders in their red coats. And the hounds were kenneled off to the side, ready for release. It seemed like everyone was waiting on them, which Liv could tell was making Mel even more nervous.

"Maybe we should just be hill toppers today," Liv offered up to Mel. "We could watch the hunt from the sidelines instead."

"Maybe," Mel said, struggling to get her foot into the stirrup again. "I'm not sure I'm cut out for this. But at least I'm dressed the part, right?"

Liv laughed. "You do look like a right proper Brit

in your Hunter Wellies," she teased. She'd loaned Mel her old riding habit for the hunt, and Mel looked drop-dead gorge in the fitted black coat and tan britches, with her hair pulled back under her velvet riding cap. Now, if only she could sit on the horse . . .

Mel made another attempt to pull herself up into the English saddle and slid back down to the ground. "What is up with these saddles? I don't stand a chance of hanging onto this little scrap of leather. Aren't they supposed to have a horn or something attached?"

"That's Western saddles," Pierce said, laughing. "Here, it just takes practice." He slipped his hands around her waist and lifted her, successfully this time, into her saddle as she blushed. "Sitting on the sidelines is a dead bore," he said. "I'll help you along, and we can lag behind the others."

"Okay," Mel said, "but don't say I didn't warn you."

"All right, let's give it a go, then," Liv said, happy that Pierce and Mel seemed to be getting on so well, and even happier that she wasn't alone with Pierce under the scrutiny of her mum and dad and Lord Northam.

They took their places at the back of the riders and within seconds, the bugle sounded and the Master called

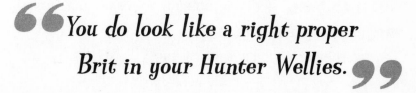

" You do look like a right proper Brit in your Hunter Wellies. "

out "Tally-ho!" In a mad rush, the foxhounds flew out of the kennel barking and racing through the wide open fields, with the riders following at a gallop.

Liv reigned Goo-Goo in so he would start off at a gentle trot, and Pierce and Mel followed.

"Hey, this isn't so bad," Mel said, even though she was listing precariously to one side of her saddle. "But . . . um, how do you stay on?"

"Posting," Pierce said. "Use your legs, like this." He demonstrated how he could move to the rhythm of the horse by holding himself up out of the saddle.

Liv giggled as Mel tried it. "Well, that's *almost* like posting."

The rest of the riders had already disappeared over a hill in the distance and all they could hear of them was the fading yapping of the dogs and the "halloahing" of the hunt staff, so Liv relaxed into her ride. Their slower pace was nice, because she could actually enjoy the crisp wintery air and the woodlands around them. With Mel along, this was way better than any hunt she'd ever been on before. The three of them talked and laughed as they rode along, and Liv had no idea how much time had passed before they finally spotted the other riders crossing through a field a few hundred yards in front of them.

"Liv," Mel said, "I thought you said real foxes weren't used in this hunt."

"They're not," Liv said. "Why?"

"Because the dogs are chasing one!" Mel cried, pointing to a small red fox making a mad dash for the forest as the hounds raced after it.

"Bloody hell," Pierce said, frowning. "Sometimes when the hounds are following a trail scent, they pick up the scent of a live fox in the wild. There's nothing to be done to prevent it, but I'm sure my father will call in the hounds before things get out of hand."

"But what happens if the hounds catch up to the fox?" Mel asked, horrified.

Liv knew the answer to that, but after exchanging a knowing look with Pierce, decided it was best not to share the awful details. Still, Mel got the hint.

"Oh, I can't watch," Mel said tearfully. "Can . . . can we just go back to the stables, please?"

"Yes, let's," Liv said hurriedly, feeling awful that she'd promised Mel a peaceful hunt that was turning out all wrong. Mel had been such a good sport about this whole day; the least Liv could do was spare her this.

"There's a road to our right that we can take back," Pierce said, casting a sympathetic glance at Mel. "It'll be faster."

But just as they'd gotten the horses onto the road, a truck drove by, suddenly backfiring with an ear-splitting bang. And before Liv or Pierce could grab his reins, Ellison reared and shot off through the brush at a full gallop with Mel.

"This was no laughing matter."

"Yikes!" Liv cried, starting off after her. "She'll never be able to stay on!"

She and Pierce flew after her, but Mel was already headed straight for the hunt riders, screaming and clutching Ellison's mane to hang on. Before Liv and Pierce could catch up, she'd run right in front of the Master and in between the fox and the hounds, sending the hounds scattering chaotically, and the fox scooting straight into a burrow, where he disappeared from view. But Ellison didn't even slow down. Instead, he headed straight for the high hedges marking the end of Lord Northam's property. For a second it looked like he was going to jump, but then he stopped dead just before the hedge, launching Mel in a glorious swan dive, right over the top.

For one horrifying moment, visions of Mel's broken body lying crumpled on the ground flashed across Liv's mind. But then Mel's head popped up above the hedge, covered in mud, but laughing.

"I'm okay!" Mel yelled, taking a theatrical bow.

Pierce let out a quiet laugh as he rushed to help Mel. Liv was on the verge of smiling in relief, too, but that was until she saw her mum and Lord Northam, both dismounted and marching purposefully toward them. One look at the scowls on their faces assured Liv of one thing: This was no laughing matter.

"I'm sorry, Mum," Liv said again, for what felt like the hundredth time.

"Such inappropriate behavior," her mum said, for what was at least the *thousandth* time. "I've never seen anything like it. I just don't understand how this could have happened. The whole hunt ended in chaos, and Lord Northam, however am I going to apologize to him?"

Liv sighed. This was, roughly, how the last hour of conversation had gone. When they'd returned to Coventry Manor, Mel had gone upstairs to change out of her mud-caked habit, and Liv's mum had immediately called a family conference to discuss the afternoon's "embarrassing events." And even Liv had to admit they had been just a tad embarrassing. Lord Northam had been furious, mostly with Pierce for letting things get so out of hand. Pierce had taken full responsibility and apologized to all of the hunt guests, but Liv's mum had seen right through it all.

"Mum, I've already explained everything," Liv tried again. "The truck backfired, and Ellison went off his chump. It was all my fault, not Mel's."

"The fact remains that Ellison never would have misbehaved had an experienced rider been on his back," her dad said.

"Exactly," her mum added. "Olivia, the point is that I'm just not sure that Melanie's visit is working out. She's distracting you from the responsibilities you have with us, and we'd really hoped you'd be able to spend more time with Pierce, which is difficult for you to do without her tagging along. Since you moved to New York, you've been so caught up in your Eli friend, and in this whole trinket-making business of yours . . ."

"You mean my jewelry designing?" Liv said, fuming. If they thought that was frivolous, what were they going to say when she told them about the design apprenticeship she'd been offered at Florentina for next summer? She'd officially accepted the apprenticeship just a month ago, but she had yet to spill the news to them. She'd been too afraid they'd refuse to let her take it, and now she was certain they'd never agree to it. None of the choices she ever made on her own—friends, boyfriends, jobs—were ever good enough for her parents. And probably never would be.

"Yes, well, the bottom line is that I'm worried you're misguided in some of your pursuits right now," her mum continued. "And maybe a few days without Mel, and your other reminders of New York, will help clear your head. So, we were thinking that perhaps she'd be more

> **66 None of the choices she ever made on her own —friends, boyfriends, jobs— were ever good enough for her parents. 99**

comfortable in a hotel for the rest of the trip. Or maybe we could fly her home slightly earlier than expected?"

Liv stared at her mum in disbelief. "Mum, I can't ask Mel to leave. She hasn't done anything wrong, and I invited her here. I can't retract the invite three days into the trip."

"To be frank," her mum said, "I'm not entirely sure how much say you have in this. Mel's ticket was purchased with *our* frequent flyer miles."

Liv wracked her brain, trying to think of a convincing argument to sway her mother. Finally, she hit on one that stood a good chance of actually working. "You're right, Mum. I haven't been giving Pierce a fair chance. But I will. I'll spend some time with him, just the two of us. I'll go out on a date with him, on Saturday, if he's around."

"Well, it's good to have an open mind about these things," her mum said. "That sounds like a marvelous idea."

Liv nodded, then bolstered her courage to add, "But I'd like Mel to stay until the ninth, just like we'd originally planned."

Her mum paused, considering the idea. "All right," she said finally. "But I hope the incident today is the last of that sort of excitement we'll be seeing for quite some time."

"It will be," Liv said, but she wasn't so sure of that at all. At least she'd convinced her mum to let Mel stay.

And now all she had to do was figure out how to make her pseudo-date with Pierce fly. And she knew just who to turn to for help.

6   6   6   6

She found Mel in the grand drawing room, warming up in front of the roaring fire.

"So, what's the Bourne-Cecil consensus? Have I been banished to the rubbish heap for the night?" Mel said, half joking, but Liv could see the worry in her eyes.

"Of course not," Liv said, giving her a reassuring smile. "But I can't say the same for my riding habit."

"I really am sorry about that," Mel said. "And about everything."

"I know you are," Liv said.

"So how'd you get the steam to stop pouring out of your mom's ears, anyway?" Mel said.

Liv took a deep breath and then rushed through her next words. "I promised her I'd go out on a date with Pierce."

"What?" Mel gaped.

"Well, she only *thinks* it's a date," Liv said, "but it won't be. Not really, because you're going to come with me."

"Oh, okay, let me dig myself deeper into a hole of disapproval with your parents by being the unwanted third wheel," Mel said, shaking her head. "I don't think so."

"But I can't get out of it," Liv said. "The only way Mum's going to let me spend any time with you over the next week and a half is to let her have her Pierce-plus-Liv fantasy. But it doesn't have to be real."

"I don't know," Mel said doubtfully.

"There're only upsides to this," Liv said. "You'll get to spend time with Pierce, I'll get to spend time with you, and Mum will be off my case. Face it, you're off your rocker for Pierce anyway, and I'm dead cert he fancies you, too."

Mel grinned. "He did slip me his cell number before we left Lord Northam's today, and said he wanted to hang out again, sans horses."

"See? There you go. It's the perfect plan," Liv said. She only hoped that were true.

❧   ❧   ❧   ❧

Later that night she called Pierce, who immediately agreed to meet up with them on Saturday after she'd

❝Oh, okay, let me dig myself deeper into a hole of disapproval with your parents by being the unwanted third wheel.❞

explained everything to him about her mum and Eli, and especially when he heard that Mel would be coming along. Liv had just hung up and slipped into bed when her cell rang.

"Hey, stranger," Eli said when Liv picked up. "How's the mother country treating you?"

"The country's brill," Liv said, grinning into the phone. "The mother's a royal pain. How's New York?"

"Who knows?" Eli said. "I haven't seen the light of day since I started editing my film. I'm subsisting on an intravenous caffeine drip and H&H bagels at the moment, so forgive me if tomorrow I think I just hallucinated this conversation."

Liv laughed. God, she missed him.

"So, what do you think the chances are of British immigration allowing another half-starved tea-dumping psycho onto the island?"

"If the psycho's also a film student from NYU," Liv teased, "I'd say slim to none."

"What if he was a friend of the incredibly influential Bourne-Cecils, and he wanted to fly over for Christmas to visit his gorgeous girlfriend?" Eli said. "Would his chances improve?"

Liv stomach lurched with excitement and dread. "Are we being serious now?"

"I am," Eli said. "I was thinking of coming over for a week over my school break. I could win your parents

"Are we being serious now?"

over with my ingenious films and my absolute devotion to their daughter. I'd really like to meet them, Liv."

"I know," Liv said. "I'd like that, too." That much, at least, was true.

"So . . . what do you think?"

What did she think? That if her mum couldn't even remember Eli's name half the time, there was no way she was going to go for Eli visiting.

"I think . . . I'd love to have you come," she said, then hurriedly added, "but Mum and Dad already have loads of holiday plans. Their schedule's insane, and I'm just not sure how much time they'll—I mean, we'll— have."

"Oh," Eli said, his voice losing some of its enthusiasm. Then he brightened. "Man, it's tough dating the social elite."

"Cheeky," Liv said. "I'll talk to them about it and see what they say, okay?"

"Tell them I'll work around their schedules," he said. "I want to start looking into plane tickets ASAP."

"Okay, but it'll be tough," Liv said. "I just don't want you to be disappointed if they can't make it work."

"Jeez, if I didn't know any better, I'd think you were trying to think of excuses for me *not* to come."

Liv laughed, but her stomach churned uncomfortably at the truth in Eli's words. "You know that's rubbish."

"Sure, hon," Eli said, but he didn't sound sure. He sounded slightly wounded.

They talked for a few more minutes, and after they hung up, Liv lay awake until well after midnight. If she didn't get up some nerve sometime soon, she was afraid she'd lose everything that really meant something to her— her jewelry-making, her apprenticeship at Florentina, and most of all, Eli. But doing battle with her mum was like doing battle with a pair of too-tight heels: You could try to bend them and break them in, but in the end it was futile; they still just gave you blisters.

ⓖ　　　ⓖ　　　ⓖ　　　ⓖ

From: alexa_v@flirt.com
To: liv_b-c@flirt.com; mel_h@flirt.com
Subject: I have good news . . . and bad news

The good news: Emma was nice enough to give me one "Get Out of Jail Free" card last night when I missed curfew.

The bad news: Kiyoko might be a tad angry with me—okay, confession time—*is* über-angry with me since I forgot about her at the gala last night. *Oye.* She was plugged into her iPod when I got into bed, and this morning she was gone to school before I got up. (You know it's serious when Kiyoko wakes up *that* early.) I'll have to make it up to her somehow. Any suggestions, *mis amigas*?

Recent sightings: A chicken (live!) in the Columbus Circle subway station (who let him down there without a MetroCard, and more importantly, *where* was he going?). Jay Manuel from *America's Next Top Model* hailing a cab. And yes, the man is practically orange! Tanorexia is an illness, Jay.

Yesterday's highlights: Scoring an audition with Bjorn V, and missing curfew and living to tell the tale.

chapter four

Kiyoko yawned as she stepped off the elevator and onto the 22nd floor of the *Flirt* offices that afternoon. What had she been thinking when she'd gotten up an hour early that morning for the second day running? Sure, she was still peeved at Alexa for ditching her at the gala on Monday, but why continue to punish herself with these brutal sunrise wake-up calls just so that she could avoid seeing her? That wasn't making a point; that was just utter stupidity. Tomorrow she was snoozing it, per usual.

She tossed her bag of schoolbooks under her cube and swiveled her chair to flip on her computer. But taped to it, she found a photo of Gen's cube with a Post-it next to it that read: FOLLOW THE CLUES.

She grinned. Rad! Maybe Gen had already grabbed her a coffee from downstairs. It didn't sound like Gen, but, hey, maybe the Grinchette had been touched by the holiday spirit, after all.

"What's up, lad?" Kiyoko said when she got to Gen's cube.

Gen frowned and handed her another photo, this one of Charlotte's cube. "I'd appreciate it if I didn't have to waste any more time with whatever type of stupid treasure hunt this is," she huffed.

"Mwah!" Kiyoko blew her a kiss as she headed for Charlotte's desk, completely ignoring the snide remark, which, to her delight, made Gen even more furious. "Love ya, lad!"

After picking up other clues at Charlotte's cube, the women's bathroom, and The Closet, she made her last stop at Alexa's desk.

"Para ti, chiquita," Alexa said, holding out a gift bag.

"Hmm, is this an attempt at bribery?" Kiyoko said, not wanting to make things *too* easy for Alexa.

Alexa shrugged. "No, but I figured it couldn't hurt to throw it in with my apology for the other night."

Kiyoko reached into the bag and let out a whoop. *Oh. My. Nondenominational. God.* Inside, was a Tokidoki LeSportsac handbag, the perfect compliment to her Hello Kitty watch and her InuYasha keychain, and all her other anime paraphernalia.

"Lynn got it as a gift for the ad we ran in last month's issue," Alexa said. "Anime's not really her thing, or mine . . . so I figured . . ."

"Love it, lad!" Kiyoko said, hugging her.

"So am I forgiven for Monday, *chiquita*?" Alexa said.

"You know it," she said. "When you're an ultra-femme supermodel, just remember Kiyoko got you there, *chica*!" She bowed with a flourish. "Hey, before we get into brain-cell-depleting study mode for midterms, do you want to hit Club Suds? It just opened and I was going to go with Adele, my mate from school. The whole place is one giant wading pool. Word is it's crawling with bikini-clad celebs. You can probably score enough 'Spotteds' for the next three issues."

Alexa hesitated. "You know I'd love to, but I've got to work late with Lynn on some brainstorms for the 'Naughty and Nice' photo shoot, and then I've got to put in some serious study time for my math midterm, and figure out what to wear to the casting call with Bjorn V."

"Point heard and taken," Kiyoko said. Fine by her. She was getting used to the big blow-off. Just then, her cell beeped with a text message.

BHOLDER: Meet me in my office ASAP. URGENT!

Ach. Kiyoko grabbed her new bag. "Belle's paging. Gotta go."

She was already halfway down the hall when she heard, "Kiyoko, wait!" Alexa's head popped up over her cube, grinning. "Screw studying. I'm in."

❝ *The whole place is one giant wading pool. Word is it's crawling with bikini-clad celebs.* **❞**

"Brill!" Kiyoko grinned. "Eight P.M. Wear your bathing suit, lad. Wet and wild is the MO."

᧧   ᧧   ᧧   ᧧

Kiyoko walked into Belle's office just as Belle was saying coolly into the phone, "I don't care if the man thinks he's Gandhi. He doesn't send in his piece for the podcast by tomorrow A.M., he'll have a lot more than his so-called hunger strike to worry about." She hung up and rolled her eyes. "Artists always find a way to blame their eccentricities for missed deadlines."

"Funny . . . it's never worked for me," Kiyoko said.

Belle laughed. "Shut the door, will you? This is for your ears only, anime-girl."

"Yes, master," Kiyoko said, her ears perking.

"Ever heard of Basil Shade?" Belle asked.

"Heard of him?" Kiyoko balked, insulted. "I worship him. God of the underground. Master of EBM." He meshed synthesized music with street sounds in a completely innovative way. She'd been trying to find a downloadable file of his train whistle and taxi-honking "Hark How the Bells" for weeks without luck. It was the only holiday music she could stomach in a time where Bing Crosby blared from practically every storefront. And she was *so* sick of hearing the sugar-spun pop renditions of carols that

Gen, in all her schmarminess, had been blasting from her bedroom every night. (Even poor Charlotte was starting to look pained.)

"Well, Hades is rising from the underworld," Belle said. "I've gotten a lead that he's signing a multi-record deal with Riff, Inc. for some serious coinage."

"That's apocalyptic!" Kiyoko cried. "It'll change the face of mainstream EBM forever."

"It's about time someone broke the clichéd mold." Belle smiled. "Breaking this news in *Flirt* could herald in a wave of new readers—less conventional posers, more social-eccentric types. Bottom line, I want the exclusive with Basil, and I want you to get it for me."

For a split second, Kiyoko was rendered speechless. How could she, mere disciple that she was, have landed such a fantastic shot to join forces with this Entertainment diva? This was it—her chance to shine in all her Kiyoko Katsuda glory.

"Your wish is my command, O great one," she said gleefully when she found her voice again. But in a flash, she remembered Bishop's closed door meeting with Belle, and Gen's comment about Belle going too far into the fringe. Fringe was more Kiyoko's thing, too, but still . . .

"Isn't this sort of risky?" she asked. "Mainstream is ninety percent of our readership. What if they don't feel the Basil vibe?"

"Who cares?" Belle stared at her, challenge in

> **How could she, mere disciple that she was, have landed such a fantastic shot to join forces with this entertainment diva?**

her eyes. "You going soft on me when I need you most, girl? Without risk, there's no innovation. And without innovation, there's only monotony. We can spare the world another Britney Spears, can't we?"

"I hear that." Kiyoko nodded. Just the thought of the cheerleader-gone-bad teeny-bopper types was nause. And maybe bringing Basil into the *Flirt* world would prove to Ms. Bishop that Belle's offbeat ideas were actually spot-on.

"So quit with the angsting over the masses and get started." Belle handed over the number for Basil's PR rep. "And do me a favor. Keep this in hush mode. I don't want any leakage, got it? We haven't nailed an exclusive yet, and I don't want Ms. Bishop banking on it for the next issue until we have it in our hands."

"We'll nail it," Kiyoko said confidently. "Count on it."

But five minutes later, when Kiyoko called Basil's rep from her desk, completely jacked up, she was met with something she'd never expected: rejection.

"*Flirt* magazine," the rep repeated like he was

spitting out something rotten. "Basil doesn't do interviews for the cloned, trend-following lemmings."

"But—" *Click*.

Kiyoko stared at phone, listening to the dial tone. Harsh. What next? If she couldn't keep his rep on the phone, she didn't stand a chance of nabbing talk-time with Basil himself. So she'd have to find a way to meet Basil in person on his own territory. Hit with a lightning flash of inspiration, she grabbed her Razr phone to text Cody Sammarkand, her boyo in Tokyo. He was there working on the music for a new anime series, *Harajuku Angels*.

> **KIYoKO!!!:** Cody, u there? *Doko ni?*
>
> **DJCody:** Just finished up with
> Matsumoto-san and Kanno-san
> at the studio. *Harajuku Angels*
> is getting ready to fly, babe!
>
> **KIYoKO!!!:** Coup! Major coup! Hey,
> I need ur help. Want to put out
> an APB on Basil Shade. U know
> him?
>
> **DJCody:** Duh—EBM legend.
>
> **KIYoKO!!!:** Can u put the word out
> on the underground circuit
> with your dj buds here? I need
> a list of his fave hangs asap.
> I'm going undercover for
> in-depth research 2nite.

DJCody: I'm on it.

KIYoKO!!!: Thx! Who loves u, lad! :)

○　　　○　　　○　　　○

It was nine thirty, and Alexa was a no-show. Kiyoko tried her cell again, and went straight into her voicemail . . . again. She and Adele had been waiting and wading under the aqua lights at Suds, and they'd reached maximum saturation point, pruny-toed central.

"That's it," Kiyoko said to Adele. "We're out of here." The vibe at Suds was fab, but she had an agenda to stick to.

"I've got to get home," Adele said. "Lockdown is at ten."

"That takes curfew to a whole new level of suckiness, lad," Kiyoko said sympathetically. Her own curfew was at eleven, and she still had three more clubs to hit before then. Cody had come through and gotten her the names of the prime locales for Basil sightings, and she had to check them out tonight. She couldn't afford to wait around for Alexa anymore.

After Adele left, Kiyoko headed for the restrooms and quickly changed into a gold-sequined halter, her favorite low-rise black leather flare pants, and open-toed alligator-skin Manolo Blahniks (on loan from The Closet. Thank you, Jonah!). She made her way out into the crisp winter air, sucking in her breath against the cold as she hailed a cab. She was sliding into the back when she spied Alexa racing toward the cab.

"Kiko, *esperate*!" she cried.

A sudden urge came over Kiyoko to tell the cabbie to step on it, but then guilt settled in. Darn her conscience. She waited as Alexa climbed into the cab, breathless and tense.

"*Ay*, Kiko-*cita*, *la culpa es mia*," Alexa said. "This is totally my fault. I got stuck at the office with Lynn until seven, and then I fell asleep at the loft studying. Are you furious?"

"Waiting for two hours without a word from you entitles me to a little pout, don't you think?" Kiyoko studied the lines of worry etched across Alexa's brow. She waffled between wanting to wage a full-blown war with her and wanting to get through the rest of the night on good terms. Finally she sighed, shook off her anger, and permitted herself a small smile. "You're here now, so it's all good. Besides, I need you to help me with my mission. Are you game?"

"For you?" Alexa gave a relieved grin. "*Cualquier cosa*. Anything."

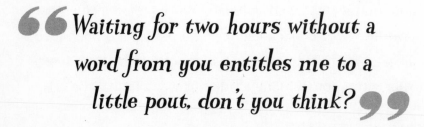

“ *Waiting for two hours without a word from you entitles me to a little pout, don't you think?* **”**

㋚　　㋚　　㋚　　㋚

"If he's not here, I'm done," Kiyoko said as the bouncer tagged her with an underage bracelet and she and Alexa walked into Heaven and Hell, the third and last club on Cody's list. No joy at the other two clubs—now it was ten twenty, and they had roughly twenty minutes to see if Basil was here before they had to get back to the Flirt-cave.

"Look at this place," Alexa said. "This *is* the underground. He has to be here."

Kiyoko took in the scene around her and knew Alexa was right. They'd literally stepped into Dante's version of the underworld. From the club's vast open center she could see ten floors reaching upward, making up the nine circles of hell, plus the apex on the top floor: heaven. They were standing in the middle of the ninth circle, treachery, where the dance floor was edged with mountains of dry ice and the booths had internal refrigerators to keep them chilled. Thrash metal blasted out of icicle speakers hanging from the ceiling. It was dark and brutal and . . . utterly brill.

"So, hell really does freeze over in New York." Kiyoko laughed.

"Where should we start?" Alexa asked. "Basil could be anywhere."

"Or nowhere," Kiyoko said. Each level was packed with throngs of dancers moving to their heavenly or hellish music of choice, and it would be almost impossible to move through the crowds, let alone search out one particular reclusive musical genius. But she had to try.

"The only way to go from here is up," she said. "Let's get started."

Over the next ten minutes, they made their way through fraud, violence, heresy, and several other floors. One had a huge open fire pit in the middle of the dance floor; another had huge fans and ceiling sprinklers that simulated a massive storm. But none of the DJs, bartenders, or bouncers had seen Basil so far. Finally, they came to a floor where manga music filled the air and people danced on an indoor meadow of fresh grass.

"I think we're in limbo," Kiyoko said. "Cody's friend Ian DJs this floor. He's the one who tipped off Cody to this place. He's our last shot."

They made their way over the DJ booth, where Ian immediately waved them in.

"So you're Cody's muse," Ian said, smiling at Kiyoko. "And I hear you had a hand in this mad-cool album." He held up a copy of the CD Kiyoko and Cody had recorded together with Matsumoto from the manga psychedelic music they'd composed. "I was just about to spin a few songs for you. Anything for the Code-man."

"*Merushi*. Thank you." Kiyoko bowed. "Any chance you've seen Basil tonight?"

Ian shook his head. "Sorry. Sometimes he goes

into hiding for awhile and doesn't show. But if he doesn't make an appearance tonight, I'll keep an eye out. Cody gave me your cell, so I'll text you if he resurfaces."

"That would be great." Kiyoko's manga-induced high deflated slightly, but at least she was getting a plug in for her music. Tonight wasn't a complete lost cause. She turned to Alexa. "Come on, lad. We've spent all night combing clubs and we haven't even set foot on the dance floor yet. Let's do it."

As the familiar music from her CD washed over her, Kiyoko relaxed. So what if she hadn't tracked down Basil tonight? There was always tomorrow, and in the meantime it was such a rush to have her own music spotlighted, she suddenly didn't care that her mission tonight had failed. She threw her head back and closed her eyes, letting the smooth chords move her body. Move it—*smack!*—right into someone behind her.

"*Sumimasen!*" she cried, whirling to face the wounded—a guy with long Goth-like hair in a crushed velvet tux jacket (complete with tails), vinyl pants, and snakeskin boots. "I'm sorry. I wasn't paying attention."

"Forgiven," he said simply and somberly. "This music. Absorbing. Moves me to a higher plane."

"You think so?" Kiyoko grinned, thrilled with the compliment. "I wrote it with a friend."

"Enlightening." He stared at her, nodding in appreciation. "It's lemming-free."

Lemming-free? Kiyoko exchanged a "Crazy?" glance with Alexa, and she shrugged. Who was this guy, and what was with all the mono-word sentences? "You know, that's the second time I've heard someone bring up lemmings in the last twelve hours. How's that for bizarre?" She laughed. "But I'm not big into lemmings, either. I'm the one and only Kiyoko Katsuda, and my music should be one and only, too. There's way too much cloned Muzak out there these days."

"You like manga psych," he said. "And trance?"

"Totally," Kiyoko said. "And thrash, grunge, EBM. It's all phat. It just depends on the artist. The edgier, the better."

"EBM. My one and only," he said, clutching his fist to his heart while Kiyoko tried not to laugh.

They talked for a few more minutes, or rather, she talked, and he did his caveman half-speak thing. But she could tell from his intense eyes that he was catching her vibes when she gushed about her music. Then he shocked her by saying, "I write music, too. Pen?"

"¡Aquí!" Alexa said, handing him a pen from her purse.

"May I?" He reached for Kiyoko's hand and scribbled something down on her palm. "Come. Visit. Sunday. Six P.M. Listen. Live." Then, he spun on his heel and disappeared into the crowd.

"¡Qué loco!" Alexa laughed as Kiyoko stared after

him. "*Ay, chiquita, vamanos.* It's a quarter to eleven!"

"We can make it in ten," Kiyoko said confidently as they rushed toward the exit. Once they were standing outside under the street lamp, waiting for a cab, she glanced down at her hand.

"Snap!" she cried. There, scribbled across her palm, was the addy and cell for the one and only Basil Shade!

chapter five

FLIRT-SPACE

Posted by <u>WriterGrrl</u> Thursday 10:02 A.M.

A short story by Melanie Henderson:
*See Mel sitting on her horse. Calm horse. Good
horse. See horse trot . . . canter . . . gallop like a bat
out of hell. See big hedge. Uh-oh. See Mel fall. Poor
Mel. See horse laugh. Bad, horse, bad. The end.*

Good thing Liv doesn't need her old riding
habit anymore, because after my run-in with
a large hedge and even larger mud puddle, it's
officially RIP—a casualty of my complete lack of
horseback-riding skills. But at least I saved the
helpless little fox from getting eaten alive. Score
one for the ASPCA!

But that was Tuesday's zenith. Yesterday and
today have been slightly more anti-climactic.
Yesterday I saw Westminster Abbey and the
changing of the guard at Buckingham Palace, but
no Prince William (sorry, Lexa!). And this morning

I toured Charles Dickens's house and the Tower of London. (Word to the wise: Never wear canvas sneaks on a tour of the Tower. Apparently, they scream gullible American! You're immediately pegged as a "yank" and "traitor to the Crown" by a Beefeater tour guide and marched to the scaffold in front of twenty giggling tourists for your beheading. Lucky for me, the acting "Queen" showed mercy at the last second and I was allowed to live, although after that mortification, I wasn't sure I wanted to.)

Liv's still tête-à-têteing with mummy dearest, so I've been touring solo (if she'd been with me, I might have been spared the Tower of Terror episode). Which means—huge benefit—I got to ogle the cute Cockney waiter at the café where I had a lunch for as long as I wanted. I do wish all four of us were here together, though. This whole Berkeley-granola-in-Queen-Elizabeth's-court persona is getting sooooo old.

Mood: Sigh!
Music: The streets of London

❀   ❀   ❀   ❀

After checking (and rechecking, and rechecking) her London street map, Mel had no doubt about it. She was completely lost. She knew she was in Southwark, along the south bank of the Thames. But where was Shakespeare's Globe Theatre in relation to the tube stop at Blackfriars and Cannon Street where she'd gotten off? Who knew? And now she'd gotten so turned around, she didn't have a clue where the tube station was anymore either. So much for backtracking.

She sighed and wrapped the vintage hand-knit scarf she'd bought at Petticoat Lane Market earlier (for five pounds! Score!) tighter around her neck and braced herself against the frigid air. All she'd wanted to do was see the Globe—was that too much for a writer to ask? The answer came in a face-numbing blast of icy wind. The sun was starting to set, and soon it would be too dark to even try to find her way through the maze of cobblestone streets.

Why was it that this never failed to happen when she set foot in a new town? She'd only been in New York for a few days when she'd missed her subway stop and ended up in Brooklyn in the middle of the night. And now London, too? And here, there was no wealthy Manhattan heiress to offer her a ride like there'd been back then. There wasn't even one black cab in sight. No, the only thing she could see was an iron-barred doorway

> **"I think I'm the one who needs some rescuing right now."**

in the narrow alleyway to her right with a sign over it that read London Dungeon. Great. Well, she was *not* going in there to ask for directions. Nuh-uh. The negative vibes alone would do her in.

She pulled out her cell and dialed Liv with shaking hands. Mrs. B-C would be annoyed that she needed help, but at this point, pissing her off was the last thing Mel cared about. But when Liv's phone went straight into voicemail, Mel made a split-second decision and hung up without leaving a message. Who knew when Liv would turn her phone on? Mel needed help now, not in three or four hours.

Then another idea hit her: Pierce. He'd given her his number. She pulled it up on her cell, and then, after a minute's hesitation, hit Send. She breathed a grateful sigh when he picked up.

"Pierce?" she said. "It's Mel Henderson, Liv's friend?"

"Mel!" Pierce said, sounding truly happy to hear from her. "Rescued any stray foxes lately?"

"No, but I'm always on the lookout." She laughed. "Actually, um, I think I'm the one who needs some rescuing right now."

"Again?" Pierce teased. "I thought I told you to stay away from those mud puddles."

"There's no mud involved this time, I promise. But there *is* a dungeon." She quickly explained what had happened.

"Well, I'm glad to hear you haven't been locked in shackles and chains yet," Pierce said. "Rescuing damsels in distress is one thing, but I draw the line at dungeons. As it turns out, I'm actually heading downtown. I'm running late for an appointment, which, sadly, isn't at the Globe. But I can pick you up on the way, and then you can join me. I think you'll really enjoy it. What do you say?"

Mel grinned. Let's see, hanging with a completely charming (not to mention seriously hot) guy, or continuing to freeze out here alone? Choices, choices.

"I say, that sounds perfect." Bring on the knight in shining armor.

ⓖ　　ⓖ　　ⓖ　　ⓖ

Must-haves for a date abroad: mood lighting, ambience, and of course, the perfect guy. Check, check, and (quick stolen glance at said perfect guy) *triple* check. Mel had it all.

The warm candlelight throwing soft shadows on the Gothic arches of the church, along with the orchestra's rich, vibrant chords, completed the ethereal feel of the evening. Mel wasn't sure if it was the fairy-tale atmosphere or the warmth from Pierce's arm brushing against hers that was giving her this heady rush. Either way, she could so get used to this.

After his driver had picked her up in Southwark, Pierce had taken her to St Martin-in-the-Fields, a beautiful eighteenth-century church just off of Trafalgar Square, for a candlelit Christmas Oratorio. They were late coming in, so Pierce had led her to a quiet corner of the balcony where they tucked away to listen. The music floated through the church with grace and passion, and Mel was so absorbed in it, she was reluctant to be jolted back into reality when the concert ended all too soon.

"That was incredible," she whispered, not wanting to break the spell of the music and candlelight just yet.

Pierce nodded. "My father thinks they're a bore, but I love them. I play the violin, too. Not anywhere near as well as those chaps did just now, but if I had more time to practice, I might someday. As it is, rugby takes up all my time outside school." A slight grimace passed over his face.

"You don't like it?" Mel asked.

❝Must-haves for a date abroad: mood lighting, ambience, and of course, the perfect guy.❞

"My father's keen on the rugby, but I'd rather be practicing my music." He stared down at the floor. "Not that I have much say in the matter, though. Not with him."

"You sound like Liv," Mel said. "I guess I'm lucky that my parents give me such free reign. But if your father doesn't approve of you playing the violin, why does he let you come to these concerts?"

"It gets him off the hook." Pierce shrugged. "He donates to a few music societies around the city, and it's one of my 'duties' to put in appearances at functions like this every once in a while. And I'm more than happy to go in his place. I fancy the music, and it gets me out of some dead stodgy dinner parties."

"I hear that," Mel said. "Just one of those parties was more than enough for me."

Pierce nodded. "Indeed. Although I found that particular party quite entertaining." He grinned at her, his blue eyes sparkling.

A thrill coursed through Mel. She could gaze into those eyes for hours. "Glad I could be there to provide comic relief." She looked down at the church floor below to see the orchestra members packing up their things. "I guess we'd better get going," she forced herself to say, even though all she wanted to do was stay.

"It's still early, though," Pierce said, checking his watch.

Mel's breath caught. Maybe he wasn't ready to say good night, either? Could the fates be so kind?

"Would you fancy something to eat?" he said. "I know a great place not too far from here, and it's entirely fish-egg free."

Mel smiled. "In that case, I'm starved. Lead the way."

ⓖ   ⓖ   ⓖ   ⓖ

"Here we are," Pierce said, stepping back into the car holding a grease-dotted brown bag.

Mel blanched, then quickly recovered with a smile. In the five minutes she'd been waiting in the car for him, Mel had envisioned a dimly-lit, intimate restaurant, or maybe a snug, comfy pub booth next to a roaring fire. She'd even guessed he'd gone to make quick reservations somewhere. But what she'd never imagined was . . . takeout?

"It smells delish," she said genuinely, silently scolding herself for having such romantic expectations. This wasn't a Jane Austen novel, after all; this was her life—Mel, the modern-day hippie who loved hummus and tofu. A life that was usually free of candlelight and roses, and fabulous just the way it was, sans frills.

"It's from Veeraswamy," Pierce said. "The oldest Indian restaurant in town. And, in my unbiased opinion, the absolute best. Especially when it comes to vegetarian cuisine."

Mel breathed in the spicy aromas filling the car as Sims, Lord Northam's driver, pulled into the traffic, and suddenly her stomach growled.

"We'll be there in ten minutes," Pierce said, "and then we can eat."

Ten minutes? Coventry Manor was at least a half an hour away. And if they weren't going back to Liv's, then where were they going?

The answer came when Sims pulled up in front of a large white amphitheater with Tudor-style beams crisscrossing the front. Mel recognized the elusive building immediately.

"The Globe!" she cried. "But how—"

"Another one of my father's donations to the arts." Pierce laughed, tucking the bag of takeout under one arm to help her out of the car with the other. "The guards owed him a favor, so I cashed in on it tonight. For the record, I'm opposed to nepotism, except when it comes to treating brill American writers to a night on the town."

Mel blushed, all of her visions of romance on the moors, or in this case, on the Thames, returning.

"Here we are," Pierce said after a guard named Mickey had let them in through the theater's side door. "Tonight, all the world's a stage, and a restaurant, too."

Mel walked into the center of the open-air theater,

taking in the beautiful stage with its deep blue ceiling painted with constellations to mimic the heavens, ornate columns, and colorful theatrical paintings. "I can't believe I'm really here," she said, beaming at Pierce. "It's so amazing that one writer could touch so many people's lives, for so many hundreds of years, isn't it? And I'll just be happy if I get a story published in the *New Yorker* someday." She laughed.

"Hey, you've got to start somewhere," Pierce said, pulling out the steaming containers of food. "Where should we eat? In the gallery? On the stage?"

Mel shook her head. "Let's do as the groundlings did," she said, sitting down on the ground in front of the stage.

They filled their paper plates with vegetable samosas, tandoori *arbi*, and *palak aloo* curry and dined under the stars in their winter coats, talking about Pierce's studies at school and his music and Mel's writing and her *Flirt* internship. The conversation flowed easily, and Mel found herself wondering at how comfortable she felt with him. Back in New York, Nick had taken his sweet time in coming clean about his feelings for her. Maybe they'd missed their moment. With Pierce, there was no guessing game. He listened to her intently and genuinely, like there was no doubt he wanted to be here, with her, right now.

She wasn't sure how long they'd been talking when she felt something cold and wet brush her cheek.

She looked up to see lazy white flakes dancing down from the sky.

"Snow," she said, laughing. "God, it never snows in Berkeley, and it hasn't in New York yet, either. This is a week of firsts for me. First time in London, first time at the Globe, first snowfall of the year." She caught a few flakes on her tongue, and then noticed Pierce watching her intently.

He brushed her hair away from her face, and for a second she thought—no, she hoped—he might kiss her. But instead he reached for her hand, which sent a bolt of electricity through her. "And your first date with a Brit?" he asked hesitantly.

"That's the best first so far," she said with smile.

@ @ @ @

Mel had thought Emma's curfew rules were strict, but that was before she returned to Coventry Manor that night to face another impenetrable and even scarier wall of maternal force: Liv and her mother. Within seconds, Mel's hottie-euphoria diminished to a meager dribble.

"Mel!" Liv cried when Mrs. Kent let Mel into the foyer. Liv and Mrs. B-C were both in wispy chiffon robes,

Mel, you've really got to work on your navigational skills.

but even at this hour Liv looked flawlessly beautiful. And Mrs. B-C would have, too, if she hadn't been frowning so deeply. "It's after midnight. We were about to call the cop-shop to report you missing. I rang your mobile at least a dozen times. Where were you?"

A dozen times? How could she not have heard it at least once? Then Mel remembered. "I'm sorry! I forgot to turn my phone back on after the concert," she said, shrugging. "But I did try calling you earlier, and you never picked up."

"We were at a gallery opening for one of Mum's friends until ten," Liv said distractedly. "Concert? What concert?"

"It's a long story," Mel said, explaining how she'd gotten lost in Southwark and Pierce had come to her rescue. And once Mel had told them everything, Liv calmed down considerably.

"Aside from the fact you nearly drove me batty," she said with a teasing but relieved smile. "I'm glad Pierce was around to look out for you. But Mel, you've really got to work on your navigational skills. You're utterly scatty when it comes to directions."

Mel started to laugh, but then noticed Mrs. B-C's frown deepening into a Grand Canyon. "Well, I hope Pierce wasn't kept from something important. I'll have to call Lord Northam right away and apologize for inconveniencing his driver and disrupting Pierce's evening plans," she said.

Mel blushed, seeing right through to the truth behind Mrs. B-C's huffiness. *She's annoyed that it was me and not Liv who spent the evening with Pierce!* Mel thought. *Unbelievable!*

"Well," Mrs. B-C said, brushing imaginary lint from her robe. "I'll say good night. It's been a rather trying evening, and I'll have to make an early start of it tomorrow, since I lost time tonight when I should have been planning for Maia's exhibit opening." With a pointed look at Mel, she swept from the room.

"So, do you want to hear what happened with Pierce?" Mel said conspiratorially to Liv.

But Liv, who'd been staring after her mom with a pained expression, just shook her head and blew out a world-weary sigh. "I really wish you'd called, Mel," she said quietly. "It would've saved a lot of trouble."

"For who?" Mel burst out, her cheeks flashing pink with sudden anger. Liv was mad at *her*? How completely twisted was that? "You've been virtually MIA for the last week, and I can't just sit around for the *next* week waiting for you to finish up with all your incredibly important social engagements."

"Bollocks! Do you think this is fun for me?" Liv said. "That it's so bloody fantastic to tag along with Mum on her schmoozing errands? I do it because I don't have a choice, Mel, not because I want to."

"But you do have a choice," Mel said. "Don't you

think it's time you stood up to your mom? I bet you haven't even told her about Eli wanting to visit, or about your Florentina apprenticeship, either. Have you?"

"It's not that easy, Mel," Liv muttered. "You've no idea what it's like."

"You're right, I don't," Mel said. "But I'm not the one who's about to lose out on a fab boyfriend and job, either." She turned to go upstairs. She was wiped from the day, and from this conversation. "Look, I came here to see London with you, but I'll keep doing it alone if I have to. Just don't get on my case for it, not when you've already made a decision about who you're going to spend *your* time with."

Mel looked back one last time before she left the drawing room, only to see Liv biting her lip to fight back tears. Poor Liv. It had to be awful to have a mother wound so tight. But the only person who could put a stop to Mrs. B-C's control-freak ways was Liv, and Mel wasn't sure that would ever happen.

chapter six

Who needed pre-calc when you could spend a Friday morning vamping for one of New York's hottest new designers? Alexa didn't, that was for sure. She'd almost pushed her mid-morning math midterm review completely from her mind. Well, maybe "almost" wasn't quite accurate. In fact, she was feeling some serious guilt at this very moment, even though she was in the middle of striking some killer poses for Bjorn V. After going to English, her first class of the day, Alexa'd convinced Mary Beth, her friend from math, to cover for her while she went to the audition.

"What am I supposed to tell Sister Claire?" Mary Beth had asked.

"Tell her that I went to the nurse," Alexa had told her, then melodramatically grabbed her stomach. "*Ay,* these cramps are *killing* me!" She straightened up, grinned, and winked. "She'll never ask any questions."

Mary Beth rolled her eyes. "You so owe me for this."

"The next round of freebie makeup I get my hands on at *Flirt* is yours," Alexa said. "*Gracias, chiquita!*"

Now, though, as Alexa moved into another pose for Bjorn

V, she worried if Mary Beth had pulled it off. And, more importantly, if she would still be prepped for Monday's midterm after missing today's review. She gave herself a mental shake to snap out of it and turned on another cover-girl smile for Bjorn V.

"And turn one more time for me, please," he said, and Alexa swiveled gracefully on cue, jutting her hips out. "Good."

The outfit she'd chosen for the audition was a no-frills ensemble of Dolce flared wool culottes, her favorite pair of black boots, and a cowl-necked burgundy turtleneck. It worked for the chilly weather at Rockefeller Center and seemed to fit in with the ambience—the ice-skating tourists in the rink down below and the twinkling lights of the ninety-foot-tall Rock Center tree. Alexa was dressed like all the other street-goers, and Bjorn seemed to appreciate her *everywoman* persona.

As she finished up her last pose, Bjorn asked, "How much more time do you have?"

"I'm free," Alexa said simply, mentally obliterating the last shred of worry she was feeling over school.

"Good," Bjorn V said. "I'd like to use you in the shoot, if that's all right."

Alexa beamed. "*Claro qué sí*. Of course!"

A sharp snap of his fingers, and Bjorn had his costume designer and makeup artist hovering at his side. Alexa nearly expected a "Yes, master" to reverberate through the ranks, but Bjorn V didn't even take the time to wait for ego-stroking, if any was to come. She could see he wasn't about pretense; he was about performance.

"Get her dressed and ready," he stated simply but forcefully. "I want crystals, feathers, but go easy on the body glitter. I don't want her looking like the inside of an ice box. She's a love affair between deep freeze and the equator. Go!"

The two gofers nodded and quickly ushered Alexa into a heated tent full of wardrobe racks and vanities. A few models were lounging around under plush shearling throws to stay warm between shots. They cast indifferent glances her way and then quickly took an ignore-her-completely stance. Alexa didn't care, though. This was her moment, and even if she was a newbie, she could walk the walk with the best of them, or at least *pretend* she knew what she was doing. It was all about *cojones*. That much she'd learned in Paris.

An excited smile spread across her face as Perry, the costume designer, appeared at her side holding a creamy ensemble that looked decadent enough for royalty, or for an Argentine cover girl.

Twenty minutes later, Alexa stepped out of the tent as a snow princess, clad in an ermine shrug, a pearl-

❝ I want crystals, feathers, but go easy on the body glitter. ❞

encrusted halter, and a silky floor-length skirt bustled with swan feathers. Swarovski crystals sparkled on her lashes and laced her forehead and cheekbones in delicate snowflake swirls.

"Yes, but not quite . . ." Bjorn V studied her with hawklike precision, adjusting her shrug so it slipped off one of her shoulders and shaking some of the crystal hairpins from her hair so her dark curls fell haphazardly around her face. Then he stood back for one more appraisal. *Trés magnifique,*" he said, giving a subtle nod of approval. "I want you front and center."

He led her over to a platform setup in front of the Christmas tree, where several other models were already frozen into poses. Alexa took her place in the center, not quite believing this was actually *her* doing this. How had she gotten here? She had *nada* idea. But then again, what did it matter? As the shutter clicked in her face, she looked fearlessly into the lens. When the other models got huffy over being repositioned, Alexa found she could almost guess where Bjorn V wanted her, depending on the angle of the camera lens and the sunlight and shadows playing over the area. She would move into a new position before he even asked her to, but each time, he nodded in approval. Working with a camera was second nature to her, and whether she was posing in front of it or snapping shots from behind its lens, there was one thing she was sure of: This was where she belonged.

Two hours and several hundred shots later, Bjorn V called it a day. Alexa stepped off the platform gratefully, stretching her stiff, chilled muscles as best she could in her tight-fitting ensemble. The rest of the models scurried into the tent, but Alexa waited, unsure of what her next move should be. After giving some final directions to his crew, Bjorn V motioned her over.

"You did well," he said. "The level of comfort you showed in front of the lens was impressive."

Alexa smiled. "I know cameras too well to be afraid of them."

"I like that about you," he said. "Intrepid without vanity or pretension. That's also what I hope to embody in my collection." He paused, then added, "I'm leaving town for Europe tomorrow morning, but maybe we can discuss future opportunities for you over a late lunch today?"

Alexa nearly jumped in her excitement, but then remembered she had four-inch heels on just in time. Future opportunities! Did that mean another photo shoot, a show, or—gulp—a contract offer? She didn't dare think about that. But wait, what about the rest of her classes? She'd already missed math and lunch, and was ten minutes late and counting for history. She knew she was already on thin ice with Mother Michael, and the rest of

> **❝ I know cameras too well to be afraid of them. ❞**

her reviews were *muy importante*. But if Bjorn V was jetting off to Europe tomorrow, when would she get another shot at this? Maybe never. No, it had to be now.

"Lunch would be great," Alexa said. School would have to wait. This was just too amazing to pass up.

ᖆ　　ᖆ　　ᖆ　　ᖆ

KIYoKO!!!: Yo chica, where r u?

Chica_snappa: On my way to *Flirt*. Just finished late lunch with Bjorn V! Ur not going to believe this! Drumroll *por favor*... he offered me a contract!

KIYoKO!!!: *Snap!* Congrats! But forget coming here. U better get your butt off the runway and downtown *pronto, chica*. Delia's put out an APB on you, and Lynn's going berserk. You're an hour late for the Naughty and Nice shoot. Remember? She's been calling ur cube for the last forty-five.

Chica_snappa: *Ay, no!*

KIYoKO!!!: I take that as a yes, you forgot. Run, Forrest, run!

After throwing her entire stash of cash at a cabbie to take her downtown ASAP, Alexa made it to the photo shoot in under fifteen. She flew through the doors of the rented SoHo loft that Lynn had booked for the shoot and frantically grabbed her camera equipment.

But even though she was in panic mode, her good mood held on. She was still on a mega-adrenaline rush from her lunch with Bjorn V. He wanted her as his top model for the launch of his first collection. She'd start shooting over the summer and into next fall, which would mean that she'd have to stay in New York for another year—¡Qué bueno! And what he'd offered was more than enough to cover her spring and fall tuition at St. Catherine's, and then some. There was no way she could pass that up. It was all so surreal, and so—so *fantastique*. She'd be smiling about this for the next week. No—the next millennium.

She stepped around the lights, camera cords, and models dressed in the vivid golds and reds of Christmas ornaments, only to come face-to-face with a pair of glowing, inferno-like eyes.

"Thanks so much for showing, but you took longer than the second coming," Lynn hissed. "Where have you been?"

Alexa opened her mouth to explain, but Lynn just held up her hand. "Never mind. I don't want to know, and

"Thanks so much for showing, but you took longer than the second coming."

frankly, I don't care. I need you on lighting . . . now."

Alexa nodded and scurried to adjust the floor lamps for the next model, left speechless by Lynn's biting remarks. Sure, she was late, but Lynn had never come down on her so hard before. She was usually more the laid-back type. So why all the hellfire and brimstone?

Suddenly, Alexa saw the reason. Walking purposefully toward her was none other than her lordship, Josephine Bishop. What was she doing here? She never came to photo shoots. And *por supuesto*, the one time she'd decided to sit in on one, Alexa was late. Bishop's hair was knotted so tightly at the base of her neck that Alexa wondered if the slightest wrong move would snap the hair follicles straining against her temple, and her bloodred vampiress lips looked ripe for a fresh kill.

Alexa braced herself as the chill radiating from Ms. Bishop's eyes hit her full force. *This is it,* she thought. *Adios al mundo.* Good-bye *Flirt* and Bjorn V, farewell Nuevo York. Hello permanent house arrest in Buenos Aires.

"Ms. Veron," Ms. Bishop said. "How kind of you to put in an appearance. Might I ask what kept you so detained during our most important shoot of the season?"

Alexa sucked in air like she was taking her last

breath. "I'm so sorry. I had a casting call with Bjorn V, and it went longer than expected, and—"

"That will do," Ms. Bishop interrupted. "Bjorn V. Well, I'm glad to hear that your lack of punctuality doesn't also coincide with any lack of taste. For a novice, attention from him is quite the *éloge*. But that being said, you also have other obligations, at school and at *Flirt*."

"I know," Alexa said quietly, suddenly wondering if Ms. Bishop knew she'd missed most of the school day. But no, that wasn't possible. Even the grand dame herself wasn't that omniscient.

"I realize you're consumed with your midterms and modeling opportunities at the moment," she said, "but a pretty face on the cover of a magazine is only fresh for a few seasons before it gets tiresome. Be careful not to let your talent as a photographer fall by the wayside in the midst of your cover-girl envy."

Alexa nodded, and when she dared to look up again, Ms. Bishop was already walking away to where Delia was waiting, a slew of messages in her hand. Alexa let out her breath in one huge rush. Well, at least she'd been spared this time. And—shocker—had Ms. Bishop

"A pretty face on the cover of a magazine is only fresh for a few seasons before it gets tiresome."

actually complimented her on her photography? *¡Triumfo!* But then again, why hadn't she been more enthused about her modeling?

Alexa knew modeling would be a short-lived career for her, but photography would always be there. Plus, how could she turn down a contract that would pay her way for the next year? The contract she'd been offered in Paris hadn't been nearly as tempting, and she certainly hadn't been about to leave New York for it. But working with Bjorn V, she could have it all: more time in New York, full-paid tuition, and more chances to work on her photography, too. She had to take this shot. Of course, she'd wait to tell her parents until after she'd finished (and aced!) her midterms. If her grades were stellar, they'd have no choice but to let her model.

Alexa grabbed her camera and joined Lynn to set up the props for the next round of shooting with a renewed smile. Modeling, photography, school—she could handle it all. Now, if only she could just find her flash . . .

☺   ☺   ☺   ☺

What have I done this time? Alexa wondered as she hurried from the depths of the Christopher Street subway station and turned onto Bleecker, making her way into the heart of the West Village. She flipped her phone open and reread Kiyoko's text message:

KIYoKO!!!: Meet me at 14 Bleecker for chats asap!

After the "Naughty and Nice" shoot, Alexa'd planned to head back to the *Flirt* offices to put in a few hours downloading her shots for Lynn. If she worked late tonight, maybe Lynn would take it as a plea for peace. Lynn had relaxed a bit by the end of the day, but she'd still given Alexa a cool good night. Alexa wanted to prove to her, Ms. Bishop, and everyone that she wasn't OOCAO (Out of Control and Overloaded). At least, she didn't think she was.

But that text message from Kiyoko had freaked her out, and now she was trying to remember what else she must have forgotten today. Had she and Kiyoko had plans that she'd forgotten about (again)? Or maybe she'd left her pile of discarded clothes from her earlier Bjorn V-induced wardrobe crisis all over Kiyoko's bed? That was a very real possibility. Whatever it was, she hoped that Kiyoko would go easy on her. After all, it wasn't like she was the most reliable person, either. In fact, usually it was Alexa who had to remind Kiyoko to stash her anime DVDs back in her room, or pick up her dirty clothes from the bathroom floor before Gen had an aneurysm. If there was one thing Alexa wasn't, it was a flake. At least, that had been true until recently. Well, whatever the reason Kiyoko wanted to see her, Alexa hoped it wouldn't mean a blow-up. She'd had such a whirlwind day, and now all she wanted to do was focus on the best part of it—the contract offer from Bjorn V.

When she reached 14 Bleecker, a wave of enticing aromas engulfed her, reminding her suddenly of Buenos Aires. She recognized the tangy Latin spices *chimayo* chile, chipotle, and cumin as she descended a tiny staircase under the street level to a hole-in-the-wall tapas bar called Valé.

"Felicitaciones!" a crowd of voices called out when she walked through the door, and she stopped dead, a smile of delight and surprise spreading across her face as she spotted Kiyoko, Emma, Gen, and Charlotte cheering and clapping for her.

"¿Qué paso?" Alexa said as Kiyoko jumped up from the table to give her a hug.

"I spread the word about your contract, lad." Kiyoko smiled proudly. "The virgin sangria's on us!" She handed Alexa a wine glass filled with sweet-smelling juice and fruit, and her Razr phone. Alexa saw two text messages saved on the screen, one from Mel and one from Liv.

WriterGrrl: Lexa. congrats! Wish we could be there with u to celebrate. Have some sangria for me.
LondonCalling: Cheers. Lex. Can't

wait to see u walk the walk during Fashion Week next to Heidi and Giselle.

Alexa grinned, handing the phone back to Kiyoko. She couldn't wait to fill Liv and Mel in on all the details of what had happened today. She wished they could be here, too, but they'd be back in town soon enough.

"We're so proud of you!" Emma said, leaning over the table to give Alexa a hug. "It's not every day we have a future supermodel residing at the Flirt-cave."

"Not a supermodel yet," Alexa said, "but thanks for the vote of confidence."

Charlotte offered heartfelt congratulations, too, but Gen was a lot more subdued.

"Maybe we'll be working the modeling circuit in New York together," Gen said. "I just gave my portfolio to Prada last week."

Kiyoko rolled her eyes. "And did they tell you they were already stocked up on munchkins?"

Gen shot daggers at Kiyoko with her eyes, while Alexa tried not to giggle and Charlotte looked uncomfortable. "Presence on the catwalk isn't about height," Gen said huffily. "It's about poise."

"*Es verdad,*" Alexa said, trying to appease Gen so they could all enjoy the night.

And thankfully, Gen dropped the subject as the

waiter appeared armed with half a dozen small plates full of *picadas*, Argentine appetizers. Alexa's mouth watered as a feast of empanadas, *mollejas*, chorizo, cheese, and olives were set on the table.

"*Muy de la banana,*" she said, filling her own plate with a hearty sampling.

Everyone dug in, but Gen quickly lost her appetite when she found out that *mollejas* was barbequed beef stomach. As they ate, Alexa forgot all about the stress of the *Flirt* photo shoot and about her looming exams, until her cell rang and she saw Mary Beth's name flash on the screen.

"Lexa," Mary Beth said when she picked up. "Bad news, *amiga*. Mother Michael went to the nurse's office to check on you after she found out you were sick."

"*Ay, no,*" Alexa moaned.

"It gets worse," Mary Beth said. "She knows you never showed for your other classes, either. She checked with your teachers, and she asked me about what happened. I had to tell her, Lexa. Now she wants to see you after midterms are over." Mary Beth sighed into the phone. "I'm sorry. I tried."

" Maybe we'll be working the modeling circuit in New York together. I just gave my portfolio to Prada last week. "

"That's okay. *No te preocupas*. Don't worry," Alexa said automatically, even though her heart was filling with dread. She hung up and stared at the food on her plate, suddenly feeling the urge to push it all away. She couldn't blame Mary Beth for this. Nuh-uh. This was all her own fault, and she'd just have to deal with Mother Michael, and whatever punishment she had in mind.

"Alexa, everything okay?" Emma asked, concern in her eyes.

Alexa shook off her worry and brought the smile back to her face. "*Sí, todo está bien*. Everything's fine." For tonight, she could forget all about Mother Michael and her finals. Right now, it was fiesta time with her *amigas*, and nothing was going to keep her from enjoying that.

chapter seven

FLIRT-SPACE

Posted by <u>KIYoKO!!!</u> Saturday 11:13 A.M.

Liv and Mel—How goes it in the mother country? Missed you at Lexa's party last night. I'm prepping for my meeting with the great and powerful Basil Shade tomorrow. Why does the man speak in two word sentences? Must explore.

RUMOR: Unconfirmed. Is Head Diva Bishop really battling Belle the Bosso Magnifico? Or is Gen harboring delusions of bringing down Kiyoko and friends? My instinct tells me Gen is just on a rampage.

Mood: Invigorated. Things are happening!

Music: EBM, Basil Shade-style. Finally downloaded "Hark How the Bells." Am one with car horns and synthesized symphonies. Music of chaos and crazed holiday shoppers.

⟳　　⟳　　⟳　　⟳

Liv was a dead awful liar. Just the thought of lying, especially to her mum of all people, turned her stomach sour. But this was the only way she could think to make things up to Mel after their fight on Thursday. She hadn't been able to get out of a Friday appointment with her mum at the caterer's, planning out the menu for the Tate ball, but she was determined today, Saturday, would be just for Mel. And that was why she found herself getting up an hour early to join her mum and Alyse, her assistant, for tea and scones in the atrium to put her plan into action. Of course, she was just short of tossing her scone *and* her tea, but if she could make it through this, she stood a shot at having her whole day gloriously Mum-free.

"So," her mum said to her as she finished up her tea, "this morning you'll join me and Alyse at the Tate to view the entertainment space for the ball. The special-events coordinator has assured me that the exhibit hall has ample space for at least a hundred, but I will not have people packed in like sardines. Our guests must be able to view Maia's artwork with ample breathing room for reflection."

Liv glanced at Alyse, who was scribbling notes,

66She'd loathed every second of it, but she'd pulled it off. 99

then took a deep breath and dove right in. "Um, Mum," she said hesitantly. "Actually, I'm not sure I can join you today. Pierce called, and he wants to make an earlier start of our date, so that we have the whole day together."

"Well, well," her mum said, a pleased smile playing on her lips. "How delightful."

"Of course," Liv said, wanting to play up the responsible daughter bit, "I can tell him no if you really need me, but—"

"Nonsense," her mum said. "He must be planning something very special for the two of you to do. It would be quite indecent to disappoint him. I'm sure Alyse and I can handle the planning today."

"Of course we can," Alyse said, smiling conspiratorially at Liv's mum, like the two of them were experts at this little matchmaking scheme.

"Really, Mum?" Liv said, showing genuine enthusiasm as the delish idea of freedom unfolded before her. "Thanks."

Liv's mum stood up from the table with Alyse and patted Liv's cheek affectionately. "You just enjoy your day and have fun, darling. I can't wait to hear how it goes." She and Alyse headed for her office, but she turned once more to beam at Liv. "Kisses."

As soon as her mum disappeared, Liv stood up from the table on quivering legs. Well, she'd loathed every second of it, but she'd pulled it off. And now all she had to do was be patient, and as it turned out, she didn't have long to wait.

As soon as she saw Giles pull out of the drive with her mum and Alyse at ten, she rushed to Mel's bedroom.

"Liv, I'm sleeping here," Mel grumbled as Liv whisked the drapes back so that the bright morning light hit Mel square in the face.

"Not anymore," Liv said. "Look, I know it's been tough for you to be on your own this week, but I've managed to get out of Mum's plans for the day."

"Well, will wonders never cease," Mel said, pulling the covers over her head.

"Oh, shut your face," Liv said playfully, ignoring Mel's dry comment and yanking the covers back. It wasn't like Mel to be sarcastic, but Liv guessed she was still raw from Thursday. "The point is, we have eight hours before we meet Pierce for dinner. Eight hours to do whatever we fancy."

Liv let this sink in, and finally Mel sat up in bed, smiling. "Why didn't you say so? Let's go."

�‌ᓂ   ᓂ   ᓂ   ᓂ

"I must be in heaven," Mel said dreamily as she took in row upon row of rare book shops and antique stores on the narrow, cobblestone street.

"Sorry to disappoint," Liv teased, delighted to see the wide smile on Mel's face, "but this isn't heaven. It's Cecil

"We've got a disapproving audience. Namely, your mother."

Court. But I suppose for a writer, it would come in a close second."

After a morning touring Kensington Palace, Liv had hit on the idea of bringing Mel to this part of London, hoping that Mel would appreciate the quaint atmosphere and the thousands upon thousands of rare and antique books to be found in the stores here, and, thankfully, she'd been spot-on.

"Is that . . . is that Charing Cross Road? As in the book *84, Charing Cross Road*?" Mel asked in a hushed whisper, like she was saying something holy, pointing to the cross street intersecting Cecil Court.

"Indeed," Liv said.

"Omigod," Mel squealed. "I love that book. I used to fantasize about carrying on an overseas epistolary love affair just like Helene Hanff and Frank Doel. Of course, they never really had an affair, but just think if they'd been in the same place together."

"Pardon, Mel, but you've met your overseas chap now, haven't you?" Liv teased. "And you and Pierce *are* together in the same place, at least for another week."

"Yes, but we've got a disapproving audience," Mel said, laughing. "Namely, your mother."

"Who says that has to stop you from a good old-fashioned snog session?" Liv said.

"Okay, who are you, and what have you done with quiet, proper Olivia Bourne-Cecil?" Mel teased.

"I'm getting a bit weary of the proper part, really," Liv said.

"Glad to hear it," Mel said, pulling her toward the first bookstore on the left, Tindley & Chapman. "Come on, let's see if we can find you a copy of *Lady Chatterley's Lover* to spice things up for you and Eli, then."

"Cheeky!" Liv cried, giggling.

For the next few hours, they popped in and out of stores along the street, buying some perfect gifts for Kiyoko and Alexa at one hole-in-the-wall antique shop, stopping in for tea and a poetry reading at Omega Books, and finally finishing up at the last bookstore in the long line, PJ Hilton.

They walked into the musty-smelling bookstore and were immediately lost in a maze of spindly bookcases, filled to the brim with everything from pricey first editions to worn and battered but well-loved hardcovers. Mel headed for the Social Issues section, while Liv stopped in Fashion. She was delighted to find some nineteenth-century hand-colored fashion plates from *The Englishwoman's Domestic Magazine* and *The Queen*, two of Britain's oldest fashion magazines. She snapped them up, thinking they'd be perfect to frame and hang on her bedroom wall in the Flirt-cave. Then she lost herself in perusing some old books on jewelry design, and finally decided on purchasing one as inspiration for some of the new ideas she was working on for the Barney's display. She had just paid for her finds when Mel rushed up, breathless and beaming, with an armload of books.

"Are you buying the entire store, then?" Liv teased.

"Funny." Mel elbowed her. "I just couldn't help myself. There's so much here. I have to get this," she said, holding up a copy of Mary Wollstonecraft's *A Vindication of the Rights of Women*. "This was the first published feminist essay. A century and a half before women got the right to vote, even."

"Just think," Liv said. "Two hundred years from now, some aspiring writer's going to come here looking for works from the brilliant essayist and author, Melanie Henderson."

Mel laughed. "It's a nice thought."

"Oh posh," Liv said. "It's a fact. You'll make it, Mel. I know you will."

"Thanks," Mel said sincerely. "That means a lot to me. And thanks for today, Liv. I'm so glad we're finally getting to hang out, you know?"

"Me too," Liv said, smiling at her friend. She was having an ace time with Mel, and this beat out spending a dead boring day with her mum at the Tate. It may have taken her all week, but she was finally doing something for herself, and for Mel, and it felt great.

"So," Liv said. "Should we go meet Pierce at the Grey Dog Pub for your date, then?"

"Um, excuse me, but don't you mean *your* date?" Mel teased.

Liv shook her head. "The only date I fancy right now is Eli. I'm just along for the ride."

ⓖ　　ⓖ　　ⓖ　　ⓖ

Liv took another sip of her delish ginger beer, looking out on the city skyline from the floor-to-ceiling windows at Club Coliseum. The club overlooked the Thames River, and the city's twinkling lights made for a fab backdrop to the dance floor, where Liv could see Pierce and Mel moving in slow motion to James Blunt's "You're Beautiful." The two of them looked so comfortable together, and Liv could tell by the bright smile on Mel's face that she really fancied him. And well she should, since Pierce had been hanging on her every word all through their dinner at the pub and hadn't left her side once here, either. Pierce had even made sure the Grey Dog had vegetarian food for Mel, which was no small feat, since nearly every pub in London that Liv knew of served the standard bangers and mash and shepherd's pie without giving much thought to roughage. Liv was happy for both of them. After the guessing game she'd been through with Nick, Mel deserved to spend some time with a guy who was ready to do some proper courting.

"So, Liv, I don't suppose you'd fancy a dance?" Pierce's friend, Alastair, asked her as he joined her in the booth.

"Thanks, but maybe later," Liv said. Pierce had invited Alastair along so they'd make a foursome, which thankfully got Liv out of third-wheel status. And much to Liv's relief, Alastair had a girlfriend who was out of town at the moment, so the two of them had been able to ease into a comfy platonic chatter straightaway. "I'm not much in a dancing mood right now."

Alastair nodded. "Me either, but I just thought it'd be polite to ask." Liv laughed, and Alastair smiled. "Are you missing your Eli fellow as much as I miss my lass?"

"Yes, sad sack that I am," Liv said. "It would be brill if he could be here right now, but he's finishing up his semester at NYU."

"But maybe he could come out to visit after that," Alastair said.

"Not if my parents have anything to say about it," Liv muttered.

"Aha," Alastair said. "A case of star-crossed lovers, I'll wager."

"More a case of an overbearing mum," Liv said.

"Oh, right. Pierce told me all about the plotting

that went on for tonight. Seems like a lot of trouble to go through to appease your mum, though."

"So right," Liv said. And the more she thought about it, the more ridiculous the whole situation seemed. Here she was, missing Eli and in the middle of a fake date with a guy she had absolutely no interest in at all. How had things gotten so botched up? She'd meant what she said to Mel earlier. She was tired of being proper and playing by all the rules, and the last thing she wanted to do was jeopardize her relationship with Eli all for the sake of avoiding conflict with her mum. She made a decision right then and there. She'd talk to her parents first thing tomorrow and tell them that Eli was coming to visit for Christmas whether they approved or not. Pierce had already offered earlier to have Eli stay with him, so it could work. All she had to do was take a stand. She'd done it at the beginning of the summer, and she could do it again now.

"Well," Alastair said, pulling Liv out of her thoughts. "It looks like our two lovebirds are going to be busy on the dance floor for awhile. And watching all that couple stuff is going to make both of us completely morose. So, if you don't fancy a dance, how about another round of ginger beer and a game of pool? I promise you can talk about Eli all you want without me getting sick of it, as long as I get to talk about Victoria, too."

Liv grinned, suddenly feeling lighter and more

worry-free than she had in days. "Pool I can definitely handle."

And it was at the pool tables in the back of the club that Mel and Pierce found them half an hour later, after Alastair had beaten Liv roughly five times. Liv grinned when she saw Pierce's hand resting lightly on Mel's hip, and Mel looking positively delirious with happiness.

"I think we'd better get you ladies home before you turn into pumpkins," Pierce said, but Liv could see he was reluctant to say good night. "So, Liv, how would you say our 'date' went?" he asked teasingly.

"From the looks of things," Liv said, "I'd say it was a huge success. Should we go for another, then?"

"As long as you bring a friend," Pierce said, grinning at Mel and giving her hand a squeeze. "I'd like that very much."

ⓖ　　ⓖ　　ⓖ　　ⓖ

The second she walked into Coventry Manor, Liv's gut told her something was wrong. It was way past one A.M. and her mum was still awake. And from the look on her face, she was none too happy to be pacing the floors, either.

"Oh, hello, Mum," Liv said. "Er, Pierce and I picked up Mel on our way home. She was out in the city, and it was on our way." She hoped that was all she needed to say to cover her tracks and explain why she and Mel had come in together. But her mum didn't even seem to register the information. "What are you still doing up? Did something happen with Maia's exhibit?"

"No." Her mum released a world-weary sigh. "It's something much worse, I'm afraid. Something *you* already know about." She gave Liv a long, scrutinizing look.

Liv exchanged a questioning glance with Mel, who just shrugged. *Blimey,* Liv thought, *I haven't a clue what she's talking about*. What could possibly be so catastrophic at this hour?

"That Eli called for you earlier," her mum continued. "But I told him you were out on a date, so you'd have to call him back later."

Liv sucked in her breath, the world shuddering beneath her feet. Sod it. Why hadn't she seen this coming? She should have known there would be some awful mix-up after she agreed to the "date" with Pierce.

"You told him I was on a date?" Liv stammered. "But . . . Eli's my boyfriend!"

Her mum waved her hand dismissively, like this was a point of no significance whatsoever. "Well, surely you and Eli aren't serious about each other. And you *were* on a date tonight, weren't you?" she asked.

"Yes," Liv said reluctantly. She couldn't bloody well deny it, could she? "But—"

"Or did you deceive me about that as well?"

"You told him I was on a date?"

"What do you mean?" Liv asked, dread gurgling in her stomach. "I haven't deceived you."

"Eli wasn't the only one who called tonight," her mum said coldly. "You also got a call from an Emily Blanchette at Florentina. She wanted to remind you about the paperwork you needed to have signed by your parents for your summer apprenticeship. In New York." Her mum's face was a mixture of disappointment and annoyance. "Liv, how could you keep this from us? How much lying have you done since you moved to New York? I feel like I don't even know my own daughter anymore."

Liv bit her lip, fighting back tears. So the apprenticeship was what had her mum all worked up, then. What a nightmare!

"I was going to tell you, Mum, really," Liv started, "but I knew you wouldn't approve, just like you don't approve of Eli, or of my staying in New York. Nothing I ever do is good enough for you."

"Well," her mum said, "lying certainly isn't the way to prove yourself to me or your father. And given this appalling change in your behavior, extending your stay in New York for an apprenticeship is the last thing I'm inclined to do. The sooner you come home to us, the better."

In a flash, Liv's panic was replaced with fury. What right did Mum have to tell her how to live her life? Who to date? What jobs to take? She was nearly eighteen; it was time for her to take a stand. Now was her chance to be completely honest about everything. She would tell her mum she was accepting the apprenticeship, and that was that. And that she wanted Eli to come visit over the holidays, too. Yes, she'd put everything right. All she had to do was open her mouth and say the words. But when she looked at that impassable frown, her resolve crumbled.

"I'm sorry," Liv said quietly. "You're right. I should have told you about the apprenticeship before. If you think it's rubbish, I won't take it." She cursed herself for being such a wet nellie, suddenly feeling too drained to battle her mum, even for Eli's sake, and her own. "Mum, I'm completely wiped. I'll see you in the morning. Okay?"

Her mum still looked angry, but finally she nodded. "Very well. We'll discuss this again later."

As Liv made her way up the stairs with Mel, the tears finally started to fall.

"Hey," Mel said, slipping her arm around her. "It's going to be okay. You can call Eli as soon as you get back to your room. Just explain everything. He'll understand."

But Liv just shook her head. "Why can't I just tell her off, for once in my life? I'm so sick of being a doormat."

"You're not a doormat. She's just a bulldozer," Mel said with a giggle, but Liv didn't even have it in her to crack a smile. "Hey, do you want to work on some of your jewelry for the Barney's display? I can help. That always makes you feel better."

"Not tonight," Liv said as they reached the top of the stairs. "I think I'm just going to sack out. I'm done."

Mel nodded, then turned toward her bedroom. "If you need to talk, I'm here."

"Thanks," Liv said. Mel was such a sweetie, but Liv didn't even have the energy to rehash the night's events. When she got to her room, she dialed Eli with trembling fingers, but all she got was his voicemail.

"It's me," she said, her voice shaking. "Mum told me you called tonight, and I just wanted to explain everything. It's not what you think. I promise. I . . . I miss you. Call me."

She hung up, posted a quick blog to Alexa and Kiyoko spilling everything to them about Eli and her mum, then climbed into bed, not even bothering to change. The tears were falling fast and furious now, and she didn't try to wipe them away. She'd made a complete bollocks of everything, and she had no idea how to fix it.

chapter eight

Kiyoko was on her fourth Toblerone of the day. She'd held out until noon for her first one and had been steadily eating one every hour since then. She'd already called Cody twice during study breaks, but she'd still needed another restorative treatment, in the form of chocolate. It was doing its job, too—keeping her mind jacked for her Sunday cramming session. She had her bio book on the coffee table, her math book in her lap, a copy of Shakespeare's *MacBeth* balanced on the arm of the couch, and, most importantly, her iPod streaming some energizing thrash metal.

She, Gen, and Charlotte were spending the afternoon studying for midterms, with Emma providing sustenance in the form of delish homemade muffins. Alexa was at the *Flirt* office, finishing up the prints for Lynn from Friday's shoot, which she'd promised to have on her desk in the A.M. tomorrow, before her midterms. Kiyoko had saved her a muffin for later, but who knew when Alexa would be home? That girl was seriously strung out lately.

"You can't possibly be getting any studying done that way," Gen grumbled to Kiyoko from her spot in the armchair in the loft's living room.

"*Au contraire*, mate," Kiyoko said with a grin. "It's fifteen minutes on trig, fifteen on bio, then fifteen on 'Out, out damned spot!' Speed studying, Kiyoko-style." She stretched into a catlike sprawl. "I'm totally prepped for tomorrow. This is just a little extra insurance."

Gen looked at her doubtfully, but turned back to her own textbook when Kiyoko's Razr rang. She was hoping it might be Cody calling, but Lexa's name flashed up on the screen.

"*Hola*, lad," she answered. "How goes it? Did you finish your prints? Gen says she needs your help with math."

"I do not," Gen hissed.

"*Dios mio*, Kiko-*cita!*" Alexa cried. "You're late!"

"For what?" Kiyoko asked blankly.

"Your interview with Basil Shade!"

Kiyoko laughed. "Breathe, Lex. It's not until six tonight, but thanks for the friendly neighborhood reminder."

"*Ay, no,*" Alexa moaned. "Basil called the loft yesterday while you were shopping. Kiko, he changed the time from six to four. *Lo siento, pero*, I was so busy yesterday with studying and these photo proofs, I . . . I forgot to give you the message. *Andale, chiquita! Pronto!*"

Kiyoko stared at her phone, stupefied, as she processed what Alexa had said. Late for her interview with Basil! This could *not* be happening. It just couldn't.

If she missed this, Belle would go ballistic, and that was something Kiyoko *never* wanted to witness. What she said next in Japanese, she was glad no one else could understand. She snapped her phone shut without so much as a good-bye and shot off the couch with lightning speed.

"What's the matter?" Gen said with a mild smirk. "Did you forget your fifteen minutes of world history?"

Kiyoko ignored her, grabbed her coat, and was out the door, leaving a trail of Toblerone wrappers in her wake.

◉   ◉   ◉   ◉

Yabai! She was in serious trouble, and it wasn't just because she was running in platforms. Not only was she half an hour late to Basil's studio, but she didn't have her interview questions with her, either, and it was all Alexa's fault. How could she have forgotten to tell her about Basil's message? It made Kiyoko's teeth clench just thinking about it. Okay, so Alexa was under some serious stress, so what? Weren't they all? Liv was dealing with her own familial version of torture, Mel's first visit to England was being quashed by stodgy Eleanor Bourne-Cecil, and if Kiyoko didn't land this exclusive with Basil, Belle might very well trade her in for another intern. Okay, that was a slight exaggeration, but still, Belle had entrusted her with this

> **"It made Kiyoko's teeth clench just thinking about it."**

assignment, and if she blew it, there went their chance to impress Fuehrer Josephine Bishop. And there went Belle's trust in her, too.

She reached the address Basil had given her for his studio on Avenue C and stared up at the gray, vacant-looking building. *This is the place?* Kiyoko thought, taking in the dark windows and desolate, industrial feel. *You've got to be kidding me.*

But she noticed the list of names outside the door, and there was Basil's. She quickly buzzed his number and held her breath while she waited. *Please, let him still be here. Please, please, please.*

"Who calls?" a voice crackled through the intercom.

"It's Kiyoko Katsuda," she said. "The manga psychedelic girl from Heaven and Hell?"

"Come," was all she got in response, and then the door buzzed open. She hurried up several flights of stairs to find Basil's studio door wide open. And there was Basil, his eyes closed, sitting in a meditative position on a yoga mat in the center of the stark room. The only other sparse décor was a collection of speakers placed carefully around the room and a digital sound recording center and computer off to the side. The studio took minimalist to a whole new level.

"*Sumimasen*. I'm so sorry I'm late," Kiyoko stammered. "I didn't get your message until this afternoon."

Basil shrugged. "Time. What is time? Lateness means nothing in the face of eternity."

All righty then. On what bizarro planet have I just landed? Kiyoko thought, wondering how exactly to translate that into a quote for the interview.

She looked around for a chair to sit on, or a couch, or, um, a yoga mat? But Basil just motioned to a spot on the floor next to him. "Sit. Absorb. Process."

Kiyoko did as she was told, and with one subtle push of a button from a remote in his hand, Basil brought the reverberating chords of an unfamiliar song into the studio. She'd never heard anything like it before. Not from Basil, or anyone else either. Kiyoko closed her eyes and let the cacophony of city clatter meshed with synthesized bass and keyboard wash over her. The music had a scattered feel, like Fifth Avenue during rush hour, the Grand Central underground, and the Fulton Fish Market were all crashing together in glorious, mind-wrenching pandemonium. It was resonating the heartbeat of New York, and underneath

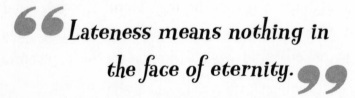

Lateness means nothing in the face of eternity.

that was a smooth, constant melody. Hard to decipher at first, but then Kiyoko recognized it as "Silent Night."

She opened her eyes as the piece ended to find Basil watching her expression inquisitively. "Thoughts?" he asked.

"Mad cool!" she cried. "The irony of combining the overbearing street noise with 'Silent Night'—it's the perfect juxtaposition. How did you do that?"

"I thought of the constant state of the city. Crisis meets calm. Serenity meets bedlam. This is New York," he said. "This is the rhythm of it."

"That is so kinetic," Kiyoko said. She got it so completely.

"Another," Basil said, hitting the remote, and this time Kiyoko recognized the undertones of "It Came Upon a Midnight Clear" alongside the banging of garbage cans on the sidewalk and police sirens. This one had much of the same frenetic pace of the last, but its combination of sounds didn't interlock with the same harmony as "Silent Night" had.

"Thoughts?" Basil asked as the piece finished.

"Interesting," she said, "but . . ." She hesitated. She couldn't believe she was actually considering offering Basil Shade a critique of his music, but then, she thought of how much she'd want a fellow musician to give her honest feedback on her compositions, so she took a deep breath and spilled it. "But it's missing something. There's almost too *many* disturbing sounds. The city's made up of so much more." She waited to let this sink in. No doubt Basil would be booting her from the studio any second.

But instead, he asked, "More of what?"

"More . . . life," Kiyoko said. "Yankees games and off-Broadway shows. What about adding in some dinner conversations between people? Or dialogue from people on the subways? Once I heard a guy belting out a Verdi aria as he walked down Park Avenue. More of the positive New York aura. You know, what makes people love the city as much as they could potentially hate it."

Basil leaned back, rubbing his temples, deep in thought. Finally, he nodded. "I see it. I hear it. I like it." He walked over to his computer, motioning her to follow. "Let's fuse," he said simply.

And for the next few hours, Kiyoko lived in Basil's world, working with him to search through his digital files, hours and hours of recording he'd done all around the city—to find the perfect sound bites to weave into his music. She watched how he channeled his creativity and asked him questions about where he'd been when he recorded certain bits, how he'd come up with unexpected combinations, how he'd gotten his start in EBM to begin with, and how the deal with Riff, Inc. had all started. Soon she had more than enough info to write one killer exclusive. Plus, he burned a CD for her of the new version of "Midnight Clear" they'd worked on together.

Time flew, and soon she realized she was cutting it dangerously close to missing her curfew. And she still hadn't told him about the *Flirt* exclusive. She had enough to write it, but whether or not he would agree to it was a different thing entirely. After all, once he knew she worked for *Flirt*, wouldn't he lump her in with all the other so-called lemmings his rep had said he loathed? She dreaded the possibility, but she had to tell him the truth.

"I have to go in a few," she said reluctantly, "but before I do, I have to tell you something. I'm not just a musician." She took a deep breath. "I'm also the Entertainment intern at *Flirt*." Oh, this was not good. He was already frowning. But she had to keep going now. "I'd like to write a piece on you . . . about your amazing music and your deal with Riff, Inc. But I need your permission first."

Basil shook his head. "No. Not possible. I don't cater to the masses."

"But it's not catering," Kiyoko said. "It's sharing with them. So maybe they don't all turn into pop-worshipping clones." Then, she took a different tack, trying to tap into Basil's wavelength and Cro-Magnon vocab. "Maybe they listen to Basil. They break out. They live."

She waited, and when Basil finally said the magic word, "Yes," she nearly screamed, but caught herself just in time.

"Basil," she said as he walked her to the door,

> **_Just like that, she had her opening line for the exclusive that would go down in Flirt history._**

"you're a man of very few words. And few syllables, too. But you are one cool cat."

"Hoka hay," was all Basil said. *Okay—English or Japanese translation, please?* She had no idea what that meant, but she was sure it was something weighty. She'd look it up online later, just as soon as she had a much-needed confab with Alexa about how she'd nearly cost her this interview.

But when she got back to the loft, Alexa was nowhere to be seen, so Kiyoko crawled into bed and booted up to decipher "hoka hay." And there it was, on the first site she looked at, a Native American expression meaning "to suck the marrow out of life." *Snap!* Just like that, she had her opening line for the exclusive that would go down in *Flirt* history.

◕   ◕   ◕   ◕

"Basil Shade could be called cryptic, or reclusive, or even Neolithic. But his music is, in one word, ubiquitous. It's everywhere all at once, in the rumblings of the subway stations, in the multilingual chatter at bodegas on the corner, in the midnight howlings of squad cars screeching through Times Square. It is the embodiment of Manhattan itself—her anarchy and her metropolitan love song."

Kiyoko looked up from her computer to stretch and take a sip of her soy latte, a smile of satisfaction on her face. She was on such a roll. She'd finished her first round of midterms this morning, and she was sure she'd aced them. Way to start her Monday! Score! Only one more day of testing to go and she'd be home free. And now her article was flowing like water from her fingertips. She was energized and in sync with the moment, until the exact second when the Bish-master blew by her cube with the brusque force of a tornado, headed straight for Belle's office.

Kiyoko craned her neck around her partition just in time to see Ms. Bishop shut Belle's door with an authoritative click. What was that all about? Ms. Bishop hardly ever graced the corridors with her presence, unless it was something of earth-shattering importance. Kiyoko's eyes flicked back to her screen, where an IM from Gen was waiting.

```
Gen_B: Watch out. Aunt Jo's on a
   rampage.
Kiyoko_K: ?
Gen_B: Belle went too far this
   time.
```

Kiyoko rolled her eyes. Gen was such a little gossip-monger, and what did she know, anyway? Still, she found it hard to concentrate on her article for the next ten minutes, until Belle's door opened again and Ms. Bishop blew out with even more of an ice blast than she'd gone in with. Kiyoko was still recovering from the chill in the air when Belle rang her phone.

"At your service, my queen," Kiyoko answered.

"Bring what you have done on the Basil exclusive into my office, please," Belle said briskly, and then the line went dead.

Kiyoko quickly printed out what she'd done and stepped into Belle's office, surprised to see her boss looking so tense that steam was practically rising from her well-exfoliated pores.

"Shut the door," Belle said, holding out her hand for the article. She skimmed Kiyoko's first few paragraphs quickly. "This is a good start, but it needs a stronger hook. More to pull the mainstream into Basil's world." She slashed through several lines with her pen, and handed it back to Kiyoko. "We're on the wire for this, anime girl.

Josephine Bishop wants a feature on Hilary Duff's new holiday album. Which I've just refused to give her for the second time in the last forty-eight hours."

"That would explain the white terror I saw in the hallway a few minutes ago," Kiyoko said jokingly, but Belle only gave a half smirk.

"She wants commonplace," Belle said. "A safety net to ensure continued readership. But we're going to give her Basil instead. Which means you've got to work faster, harder, and better. The offering has to be masterful for us to convince her to take it."

"And if she doesn't?" Kiyoko asked.

"Mort et enterré." Belle said with a short laugh. "But that's all part of playing the game, isn't it?" She stood up and slipped into her coat. "I'm off to Barney's with Trey and Lynn to check on the space for the window displays. I want you to work on the article in here. Use my computer, and keep the door shut. The last thing you need is distractions. You need to concentrate on that and nothing else."

"Consider it done, master," Kiyoko said. But once Belle walked out, Kiyoko sat staring at the remains of her article, slashed and battered, wondering what had transformed Belle from her normally calm and collected self into she-devil status. Oh well. Sometimes the holidays brought that out in people, right? It could be a case of Scrooge, the Belle Holder version. Well, a few of her sentences about Basil had been salvaged, at least, so she'd just have to rework the rest of it. She didn't want to have any part in Ms. Bishop's tirade, so she'd have to make sure the article was sheer genius, starting now.

Four hours later, Kiyoko looked up, bleary eyed, from Belle's computer to see that night had fallen. She yawned and saved the draft onto her memory stick so that she could take it home and reread it a few times before turning it in to Belle. She locked Belle's office and passed through the vacated cube farm, then stopped short when she saw Alexa, still at her desk. She was staring at her math book.

"It's a little late for studying now, lad," Kiyoko said drily, wanting the comment to have a little bit of bite. "Didn't you have the midterm at eight, or did you sleep through that, too?" Kiyoko hadn't seen Alexa since this morning, when she'd still been snoring through the alarm. She'd stumbled in last night at one A.M. after falling asleep studying at Starbucks. And even though she'd muttered an apology to Kiyoko for forgetting about the Basil interview, Kiyoko had just rolled over, ignoring her. She was fed up with Alexa's constant state of distraction lately. She knew

> **" Didn't you have the midterm at eight, or did you sleep through that, too? "**

she had a lot going on, but that didn't mean she could forget all about her fellow *Flirt*-mates in the process.

Alexa looked up, glassy-eyed. *"Tengo un probema,"* she said. "Half the test covered chapters I didn't study. Sister Claire must have talked about that in the review sessions on Friday, and I missed it."

"Too bad, mate," Kiyoko said, shrugging. "Maybe if you weren't so busy striking poses all over Manhattan, you'd have gotten it together for the test." She spun on her heel and walked out before Alexa had a chance to respond.

That night, after working for hours on her article sacked out on the couch while watching reruns of *Lost*, Kiyoko finally climbed into bed. She'd waited until long after Alexa had retreated to their bedroom to go to sleep herself. But as she crawled under the covers with her battered Picachu, she caught sight of a pile of crumpled tissues on the floor next to Alexa's bed, and a pang of guilt struck her. She tried to sleep, but as much as she tried to deny it, her conscience gave her an awful case of insomnia . . . all night long.

chapter nine

Mel woke up Tuesday morning to snow falling peacefully outside her window, the smell of fresh-baked scones floating lazily in from the kitchen, and a pale, wide-eyed psycho standing at the foot of her bed.

"Liv, why do you look like a post-feminist version of the madwoman in the attic?" Mel asked with a yawn, half jokingly, but then she noticed Liv's red-rimmed eyes and her sleepy sarcasm fell away. "Is this about Eli?" she asked.

"No," Liv said through a series of ladylike sniffles. "I haven't heard from him yet. But apparently, Florentina has heard from Mum. Emily Blanchette sent this last night." She flashed a piece of paper at Mel and shook her head. "I have no bloody say in my own life is what it comes down to."

Mel gently took the paper from Liv and read through it:

From: emily_b@florentina.com
To: liv_b-c@flirt.com
Re: Your apprenticeship

Dear Ms. Bourne-Cecil,
I was sorry to hear from your mother yesterday that

you won't be able to accept the summer apprenticeship at Florentina after all. Your mother told us that you were needed at home over the summer. We wish you the best of luck with everything.

Sincerely,
Emily Blanchette

"I can't believe she sent that, without even asking you!" Mel said, suddenly extremely thankful that her own parents were so laid-back. She gave Liv's hand a squeeze, but Liv looked completely inconsolable.

"Oh, I can," Liv said, pacing the room. "Every time I try to make decisions on my own, Mum's always intervening. You should see the disapproval on her face every time she catches me working on the jewelry for the Barney's display. I know she thinks it's all a bunch of petty tinkering on my part. And she's made such a sodding mess with Eli, I doubt I'll ever be able to make it up to him. And now there's her meddling with my apprenticeship." Her pacing was more like angry stamping now. "One way or another, she always gets her way, and I'm well sick of it."

"I don't blame you," Mel said. "But there's not much you can do about it."

"Pardon, Mel, but there is," Liv said with a determination Mel had never heard in her voice before.

> **"If there was going to be a family feud of colossal proportions, she wanted to be there with Liv for moral support."**

"I'm going to tell her off, is what I'm going to do." She nodded firmly, as if trying to convince herself. "Right now." Liv stormed out of the room, then stuck her head around the door and added, "Are you coming?"

"Oh. Sure," Mel answered, a little taken aback to be included, but guessing that Liv desperately needed the reinforcements. She leaped out of bed to follow her. If there was going to be a family feud of colossal proportions, she wanted to be there with Liv for moral support.

She'd never seen Liv so jacked up about anything, or so furious. Before, Mel had always believed she had a better chance of witnessing snow in southern California than she ever had of witnessing a tantrum from Liv.

But when Liv reached Mrs. Bourne-Cecil's office, instead of bursting in, she came within inches of the door, then stopped, and knocked firmly but ever-so-politely before going in. Mel nearly grinned. You could take the princess out of the royal manor, but you couldn't take royal good breeding out of the princess.

"Mum, I need to talk to you," Liv started out bravely.

"Olivia, this is an absolutely dreadful time," Mrs. B-

C said when Liv and Mel walked in. Her usually meticulous desk was scattered with papers, and canvases draped with cheesecloth covered nearly every spare inch of floor space in the room. "Can't this wait?"

Liv glanced quickly at Mel, who gave her a subtle nod to go for it.

"No," Liv said firmly. "It can't." She held up the e-mail from Emily and took a deep breath. "You had no right to e-mail Emily Blanchette without asking me. I know you're unhappy with the idea of the apprenticeship, but you could have left it to me to deal with it."

"Pardon me, dear, but after you kept the apprenticeship from us for so long, how could we have entrusted you with the matter of ending it?" Mrs. B-C rubbed her temples. "This way, we could ensure that there would be no more deception."

"I was going to tell you," Liv said, trying to keep her voice steady. But Mel could tell her streak of bravery was coming to a rapid close. "But you're always so ready to second guess my decisions in everything. You just make it so . . . so difficult sometimes."

> "*Pardon me, dear, but after you kept the apprenticeship from us for so long, how could we have entrusted you with the matter of ending it?*"

"I believe the difficulty here stemmed from *your* dishonesty, dear," Mrs. B-C said simply, "so don't suggest that we are at fault for this. Besides, keeping up with your studies here is far more imperative than frittering away another summer in New York, especially under the questionable influences of your acquaintances there."

Mel caught her mouth just before it fell open. Just who did Mrs. B-C think she was referring to? What were Liv's friends in her eyes, anyway, the equivalent of cheap imitation Fendi bags?

Mrs. B-C glanced at Mel, taking note of her for the first time since she'd walked into the room. It would have given Mel at least some satisfaction to see her blush in shame after that last remark, but Mrs. B-C remained cool and unfazed. "For instance, I don't know the first thing about this Blanchette woman or Florentina," Mrs. B-C said, making a masterful recovery. "Working for Josephine Bishop was one thing, but how do we know about the caliber of people you'll be working with at Florentina?"

Liv waffled. "It's not like that, Mum. Really. I just . . . what I meant to say was . . ." Her voice died away in defeat.

Come on, Liv, Mel silently pleaded, hoping to send some encouraging vibes her way. But Liv's shoulders sagged as she quickly deflated, losing her steam.

"May we move on from this, Olivia?" Mrs. B-C asked matter-of-factly. "I have much more important things to worry about right now. Alyse had to leave this morning for a family emergency, and we still haven't finalized the plans for Maia's exhibit opening at the Tate." She gave a world-weary sigh as Mel fought the urge to roll her eyes. "Thank god the invitations have gone out already, but the brochures aren't ready, and neither is the dessert menu, or the music selections. I can't possibly get everything done by Friday."

"I'm sorry about Alyse, Mum," Liv said. "But I'm sure you'll get it all done."

"Perhaps," Mrs. B-C said, looking at her Cartier watch, "but not without your help. I have appointments with the caterer and conductor today, and I need you to come along. You can help me solidify the hors d'oeuvres and cocktail hour entertainment, at least."

"But, Mum, I have to finish up my jewelry for the Barney's display," Liv tried.

Mrs. B-C waved her hand dismissively. "That can wait. Of all people, Josephine will understand the pressing nature of planning this event."

Liv was so forlorn that Mel could see she didn't have the strength or will to resist. She almost didn't believe what came out of her own mouth next. "I'll go, too," she offered, smiling encouragingly at Liv. It was the least she could do to keep Liv from going postal until she could figure everything out with Eli and the apprenticeship. "I can always taste-test any veggie hors d'oeuvres."

Despite her glassy eyes that threatened tears, Liv gave a small but grateful smile.

"I'll just need fifteen to change," Mel said.

She was already out the office door and starting up the stairs when she overheard Mrs. B-C. "It's best if Melanie stays here today," she was telling Liv. "I can't have you fretting over her all day when *I* need you. She'll just distract you."

"But, Mum," Liv started, "she's offering to help . . ."

Mel froze, making a split-second decision. The last thing she wanted to do was cater to Mrs. B-C's wishes, especially after the way she'd been treated since she'd gotten here. But then she had a brainstorm. She might have a way to prove once and for all that she wasn't the granola-crunching simpleton Mrs. B-C thought she was. And, if it worked, the plan could help Liv get through the rest of this week, too. Suddenly, she knew what she had to do.

She stuck her head around the office door and, faking oblivion, said, "You know what, Liv? On second thought, I think I'll stick around here today, if that's okay with you. I need to work on my 'Brit Fashion UnThamed' write-up for Ms. Bishop for the 'Naughty and Nice' issue, and it's going to take me most of the day."

"What a wonderful plan, dear," Mrs. B-C said to Mel. "No doubt those pieces you write for Ms. Bishop require quite a lot of revising and editing. It's lovely to see your willingness to put forth solid effort to hone your skills."

Liv sent Mel a silent apology with her eyes, but Mel just smiled reassuringly, not wanting to stress her out even more. Liv had struggled with enough battles this morning, and even though she didn't have a warrior spirit and still hadn't changed her mom's mind, Mel was proud of her for making the effort. Maybe it was the start of a braver, more independent Liv. Anything was possible, and Mel hoped it could really happen, for Liv's sake.

"I'll see you later," Mel said to her, then hurried to her room, anxious to put her plan into action. By the time she'd showered and dressed, Liv and Mrs. B-C had left for the day, so it was time for Mel to get started. Armed with her laptop, she went back down to Mrs. B-C's study, and after a quick search, found her notes on Maia Cardinale's artwork for the Tate exhibit. Next, with delicate fingers, she carefully raised the cheesecloths on the two dozen canvases until each of Maia's vibrant paintings revealed itself. Then, she sat down on the floor so that she was surrounded with the colors, textures, and moods of the collection, opened her laptop, and began to write.

ⓖ   ⓖ   ⓖ   ⓖ

"Maia Cardinale captures a life's essence in her work. The ruby, jade, and azure hues that pour from her palate are as luminescent as the holiday lights, ornaments, and decorations that adorn the city streets this time of year, and her soft lines are as comforting as the heart's glow. Her paintings are truly singular, and will leave you with a warmth that will long outlast the starkest chills of winter."

Mel reread the last paragraph one more time, then unfolded her long legs across the carpet and stretched out the cramps that had settled into them. Then she glanced up at the clock over the mantel. Five thirty P.M. She'd been working almost nonstop for the past five hours (save for a few very anticlimactic kitchen raids . . . wasn't there anywhere a girl could find a decent veggie sandwich in this country?). Now her piece was finally finished, and it was good. At least, *she* thought it was good. But she still had to get it past the world's harshest critic.

She laid the three-page printout on Mrs. B-C's desk and then gave the room a once-over. Maia's canvases looked like they'd never been touched, and everything in the office was back in place. She trudged upstairs to wait for Liv and Mrs. B-C to get home, trying to shake herself out of the wooly haze she always got into after a mega-writing spree. She was in such a blur as she flopped onto her bed that she barely registered her cell ringing in her pocket.

"Mel?" said a voice with a disarmingly cute Brit accent.

"Hang on, I'm not sure if she's present in-body at the moment or not," Mel said jokingly.

Pierce laughed. "Well?" he asked after a few seconds.

"Her brain has turned gelatinous, but other than that, she's here," Mel decided.

"Good," he said, "then she won't be of sound mind enough to reject me when I ask her out for this Wednesday, will she?"

"She's weakening as we speak," Mel said, smiling.

"How does a tour of Hampton Court, followed by a dinner cruise on the Thames sound?" he asked.

"Brill," Mel said, just as she heard footsteps trudging down the hall, followed by Liv, looking bone-tired, dragging herself through Mel's door. "Um, Pierce, I have to go. I'm dealing with a manor in crisis here."

"Sounds terrifying," Pierce said. "Give Liv my condolences."

"I will," Mel said. "See you Wednesday." She hung up and turned to Liv. "What happened to you?" Mel asked.

"I look that horrid, do I?" Liv mumbled.

"Would you hurt me if I said yes?" Mel teased. Liv could always pull off a shower-

"I'm dealing with a manor in crisis here."

fresh look even after an all-nighter studying, but right now her face was the perfect match for the gray marble mantle behind her.

"It was awful," Liv said. "Two hours discussing paté and caviar, three weighing the benefits of Mozart versus Brahms. Mum isn't just maniacal, she's a masochist."

"You'll get through it," Mel said. "Hey, any word from Eli?"

Liv bit her lip, her eyes immediately filling. "None. I sent him a long e-mail this morning and called him twice. I can't risk calling him again without looking like some warped version of *Fatal Attraction*, so I just have to wait it out."

"He'll call," Mel said. "And in the meantime, hopefully your mom will decompress some."

"She'd need years for that, not hours," Liv said just as there was knock on the door and Mrs. B-C walked in, an expression of confusion and relief on her face.

"Melanie, did you write this commentary on Maia's work?" she asked, holding up the sheaf of papers Mel had left on her desk.

Mel nodded, her heart thumping. This was it. She

66 *Two hours discussing paté and caviar, three weighing the benefits of Mozart versus Brahms. Mum isn't just maniacal, she's a masochist.* **99**

was either going to finally make some headway with the Bourne-Cecils or solidify herself in their bad graces. "I thought you might be able to use some of it for the exhibit brochure," she said, "if you like it?"

Time ticked by painfully as Mrs. B-C skimmed over the pages once again.

"It's quite . . . tasteful, actually," she finally said haltingly, as if giving praise was as foreign to her as discount designer clothing stores. "It needs some reworking, of course, and you use the word 'erudite' far too many times. But some of it might be . . . useful."

"I'm glad." Mel smiled in relief. It wasn't exactly a compliment, but it was as close to one as she was likely to get from Mrs. B-C.

"I'll mark it up this evening and then you can make the changes, and I'll have Giles run it to the print shop first thing tomorrow." Mrs. B-C turned to leave, but then paused, her hand on the doorknob. "Thank you," she said, barely audibly, then shut the door.

Mel and Liv looked at each other and burst out laughing.

"Goodness, Mel," Liv said, "I can't believe you went to all that trouble. What about your feature for Ms. Bishop?"

Mel shrugged. "It's almost finished, and I can proofread it tomorrow. I just wanted to help."

Liv hugged her. "Thanks." She giggled. "The look on Mum's face was hysterical."

"That's one small victory for Mel, one giant leap for plebe-kind," Mel said with a triumphant grin. "Now if we can just figure out a way to convince her to let you do your apprenticeship and work things out with Eli, we'll be set."

"First things first," Liv said. "Fridge raid. I bought you some tofu at Harrod's food market."

"Now that is the best thing I've heard all day," Mel said. "Your mom's 'thank you' excepting."

chapter ten

Alexa bit into one of Mami's homemade empanadas, the kind she made every Christmas. She was home again, in the beautiful Argentine summer sunshine, waiting to unwrap her presents. Midterms were over, and she was relaxed and happy with her *familia*. And there was Sister Hazel, eating an empanada in a bikini—*in a bikini? Ay, no!* What was her bio teacher doing in Argentina, in a two-piece? And why was everything suddenly shaking?

"Ms. Veron," a faraway voice said. "If you would be so kind as to grace us with your *waking* presence."

Alexa blinked and squinted in the bright fluorescent light as Sister Hazel continued to shake her shoulder. *"Qué?"* she said, to a smattering of giggles from students who were leaving the classroom.

"Well, I haven't killed a student with a midterm yet, so I'm relieved to see you rejoining the living." Sister Hazel peeled Alexa's test out from under her arms. "Time's up, and you're wanted in Mother Michael's office now. She asked that you join her as soon as your last midterm was over."

"But, *esperate*," Alexa said with growing panic, and not just because of the impending doom settling over her at the mention of Mother Michael. How many questions had she answered before she'd gone comatose? She thought she'd gotten through almost all of them, but then again, everything was one big blur, which she supposed came from staying up for the past thirty-six hours straight. It *was* still Tuesday afternoon, wasn't it? Or had a whole day escaped her somehow? "Can I just answer one more question?"

Sister Hazel shook her head. "I'm sorry, but I'm sure you did the best you could." A rare smile fleeted across her lips. "Now try to get some sleep tonight, okay?"

Alexa nodded, then with a resigned sigh walked as slowly as possible to meet her fate with Mother Michael. She knew a lecture was coming her way after she'd ditched her reviews last Friday, but she hoped that would be the worst of it.

She was so wrong.

"Thank you for joining us," Mother Michael said solemnly after Alexa took a seat in her office.

Us? That didn't sound good at all. Alexa glanced around the room looking for the firing squad, but didn't register anything out of the ordinary until her parents' voices crackled through Mother Michael's speakerphone.

"*Hola*, Alexa," her papi said, without even a spark of his usual cheeriness, and Mami sounded even unhappier. *Aye aye aye*. If Mother Michael was confabbing with her *padres*, it could only mean one thing . . . she was in way worse trouble than she'd thought.

"Ms. Veron, I called your parents to discuss the disconcerting change in academic performance you've made in the last several weeks." She flipped through a sheaf of papers on her desk, and Alexa recognized her own handwriting with rising dread. "Your grade on your math midterm was less than exemplary," she said, handing Alexa the paper.

Alexa stared at her test, which was so littered with red marks it looked like it had been through some kind of St. Catherine's chain saw massacre. And there it was, the glaring "D" at the top—a nightmare in letter form.

"Because the midterm was roughly thirty percent of your math grade," Mother Michael said, "and you had a marginal C before this, you'll be ending this semester with a D." She sighed. "Ms. Veron, it doesn't give me even the remotest pleasure to fail students, but you've given me no choice. Since you missed your reviews last Friday, you've lead me to believe that you are indifferent, if not careless, with your studies."

> ❝ Her test was so littered with red marks it looked like it had been through some kind of St. Catherine's chain saw massacre. ❞

"No es verdad!" Alexa said. "But that's not true. I do care, and I had a good reason for missing the reviews."

"Ms. Veron, if you're referring to your modeling, I'd hardly call that a good reason."

Alexa gaped at Mother Michael. "How did you . . . who told you that?"

"I called the *Flirt* offices yesterday and spoke to Ms. Bishop, thinking that perhaps your internship was putting a strain on you and affecting your schoolwork," Mother Michael said. "Ms. Bishop assured me that the internship wasn't the problem, but your contract offer from Bjorn V might be the issue instead."

Dios mio, this is it, Alexa thought. No more *Flirt* internship, no more Nueva York, and no more contract. Now that her parents knew about the contract and her grades, they'd ship her straight back to Argentina permanently.

"You know how we feel about your modeling," her mami interjected, her voice warbling with anger and disappointment. "How could you consider this contract without telling us?"

"I was going to tell you, Mami," Alexa tried, "after my midterms were over. I thought if I aced them, you might let me take the contract. It's enough to pay for my

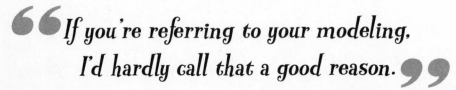

If you're referring to your modeling, I'd hardly call that a good reason.

tuition for next year and room and board."

"Well, ace them you did not," Mother Michael said.

"*Lo siento,*" Alexa whispered. "But I can get help with math from Kiyoko and Liv. They're both great at it. And maybe I can get a tutor for my other classes. Or Mary Beth can help me." She looked at Mother Michael for help, but the nun just sighed and shook her head.

"You can't expect us to support your modeling career at the expense of your studies," her papi said. "There won't be any contract, you can count on that."

"But if you'd just give me one more chance," Alexa appealed. "I'll get better grades. I promise. *Por favor,* Papi, I'll never get another chance like this with a designer like Bjorn. It's a once in a lifetime shot."

"You have a long life ahead of you," her mami said. "You'll have many opportunities like this. But your education comes first right now. Nothing else matters."

"We'll wait until the rest of your midterms have been graded," Mother Michael said to her, "and then we'll discuss your future at St. Catherine's. And now, your parents and I have a few things to finish up. You and I will talk again later this week."

Alexa nodded and stood to go, feeling the tears she'd been holding back building into a tidal wave.

"We'll call you later tonight, *mija,*" her mami said as Alexa left the room, and Alexa thought she sounded less angry now, and more worried. But she couldn't say good-bye. She couldn't say anything. The wave had crashed, and no words would come through the tears.

ᕀ   ᕀ   ᕀ   ᕀ

She'd always thought that warm churros and sweet *alfajores* were the cure-all for anything, but after downing some from the international food market in the Grand Central underground, Alexa realized they were failing miserably in the comfort food department. Now her stomach was uncomfortably full as she sat on a bench in a dimly lit corridor in the Museum of Modern Art, and it wasn't doing a thing to make her feel better. Neither was Dashal Kole's *Naked Light* experimental photography exhibit. She'd been dying to go to this exhibit ever since it opened two weeks ago, but she couldn't even get psyched about it. The stark photos played with falling shadows and shafts of sunlight, using them to illuminate or distort faces, trees, and even children's toys. They definitely matched her morose mood, but somehow that just pulled her deeper into it.

"Okay, Grim Reaper, step away from the dismal photographs and come into the light," a familiar voice said from behind her.

Normally Alexa would have laughed at Kiyoko's dry humor, but instead, she just scooted over on the bench to make room for her, without shifting her eyes from the photos on the wall.

"What, not so much as a hello after I went to all this trouble to track you down?" Kiyoko teased, elbowing her. "Come on, lad, here we've been thinking Mother Michael was holding you hostage since you never showed at work. Ms. Bishop even called her to check, if you believe that. I think she was genuinely concerned, at least as much as her slightly defrosted heart allows her to be. And Lynn was getting all OCD in your cube looking for your calendar to see where you might be. So they recruited me to go look for you." She pulled a Pokémon Pez from her Tokidoki bag and offered Alexa one, but Alexa just shook her head.

"How did you know I'd be here?" she finally asked.

"Blimey, Lexa, it's Dashal Kole. You've been lusting after this exhibit for days. You even asked Gen if she wanted to come with you to see it, remember? The act of a truly desperate *chica*. And now that I've seen his work, I get it. Totally dark, but cathartic." She popped a Pez into her mouth. "So, why the ix-nay on ork-way?"

Alexa shrugged. "I just couldn't deal. Not today."

"Well, you don't have much of a choice, lad," Kiyoko said. "What the Bish-master wants, the Bish-master gets, so come on. I know you've had an überharsh day, but you can angst over it tonight. We have to get back."

"Nunca," Alexa said. "I'm not going."

Kiyoko frowned. "I'm serious, Lex. Jared's waiting with the *Flirt* car outside, and I left Belle and Ms. Bishop arguing over the design for the Barney's display. Belle wants something resembling an S&M Christmas, and Ms. Bishop's afraid the Dooney & Burke crowd will faint dead when they see it. A full-fledged battle of the scrooges is about to ensue, and I'm here with you, so you better be grateful."

Alexa stared at Kiyoko, her fury flaring. Why did it always end up being all about Kiyoko? Even when she stuck her neck out for you, she never let you forget it. "Can you just leave me alone? I already told you I'm not coming. I don't care if Ms. Bishop fires me. My parents are probably going to make me go back to Argentina, anyway." She glared at her. "But that's something you'd never understand. You get off so easy all the time. You miss curfew a dozen times and Emma forgives you; your parents have never threatened to send you home; and no matter how many times you've messed up at *Flirt*, you always have some excuse that gets you out of it. You're probably happy my parents won't let me take Bjorn's contract. After the way you acted in Paris, you must secretly love to see me fail."

Kiyoko stood up in a flash, her eyes sparking with anger. "You think I have it easy, lad?" she said. "How about the fact that my boss and Ms. Bishop are feuding four days before the unveiling of our Barney's display, and

I'm stuck in the middle? If this exclusive about Basil Shade doesn't fly, Belle will have nothing to show Ms. Bishop for the holiday issue. And then what? You think I'll get off so easy then?" She was pacing like a enraged tigress. "And I may have acted like a jerk in Paris, but I was the one who threw you the party at Valé to celebrate your contract, remember? And you haven't exactly won the Most Considerate Friend award lately either, lad. I nearly missed my interview with Basil Shade because of you. And you ditched me at the Met gala last week and were way late showing up to Suds. I wouldn't call that the mark of a good friend."

Kiyoko swiveled on her heel, heading for the exit. "I'll tell Her Lordship and Lynn I couldn't find you, if that's what you want. But don't blame me if you're on their hit lists tomorrow."

As Kiyoko's thundering footsteps died away, Alexa's face crumpled. She rushed out of the museum just before bursting into tears. *No lo creo,* she thought. *Did I really just tell off one of my best friends?* The leaden guilt piling into her stomach answered the question for her. But she wasn't about to go after Kiyoko to apologize, either. This wasn't all her fault. At least, that was what she kept telling herself every time she thought about her cube at *Flirt,* sitting vacant for the afternoon.

chapter eleven

"Come on, Liv," a voice whispered in her ear, "the rest of the group's already left the Great Watching Chamber. Don't you want to see the Haunted Gallery?"

Liv blinked and snapped out of her daze, realizing she was the only person left in the chamber, aside from Mel and Pierce. "Pardon, Mel," she said. "I'm coming."

She followed them into the next room, trying to match Mel's enthusiastic smile with one of her own. Mel certainly seemed to be enjoying the tour of Hampton Court, alternating between snapping pics of the massive palace and holding hands with Pierce. Even Liv had to admit, the palace that had been home to Britain's royal families for more than five hundred years was an impressive place, and it had been ace of Mel to invite her to tag along on her day out with Pierce, too. Liv had told her mum that they were all going out for the day, and for once, her mum hadn't fought her on hanging out with Mel.

"You girls have been working hard to help me with the ball," her mum had said. "We can always finish up the final details tomorrow, so go enjoy yourselves today."

Liv and Mel had set out with Pierce for the palace as fast as they could, before Mrs. B-C had a chance to change her mind. Liv had been hoping getting out of Coventry Manor for the day would get her mind off Eli and her apprenticeship, but instead, she'd spent most of the morning lost in her thoughts. Since she'd been to Hampton Court at least a half a dozen times throughout her childhood, she basically had the tour memorized, down to each room and each story.

"The haunted gallery got its name from Henry VIII's fifth wife, Catherine Howard," the tour guide continued once Liv rejoined the group, letting her voice drop into a theatrical ghost-story tone. The gallery was a long hallway simply decorated with a few oil paintings and a plain rug, but it had always given Liv a chill as a child because of what had happened there. "She'd only been married to Henry for fifteen months when she was charged with adultery. She escaped from her rooms and ran to this corridor, but it was here that the palace guards arrested her. She was later executed at the Tower of London, but many say that her ghost still haunts this very spot. The specter of a woman dressed all in white has been seen on several occasions floating down this corridor, shrieking in despair and terror."

Mel shivered next to Liv. "I knew I felt the presence of a tragic soul in here," she whispered. "Creepy."

"Are you sure that wasn't me?" Liv said, only half joking.

> **"I knew I felt the presence of a tragic soul in here."**

"Still thinking about Eli?" Mel asked.

Liv nodded. "I explained everything to him in messages and e-mails, but five days with no word is like a dating death sentence."

"Sometimes a bloke just needs time to process," Pierce added encouragingly. "I'd say ring him again. He might need the reassurance."

"I'm starting to feel like a prize idiot," Liv said.

"Hey," Pierce said, "don't be too hard on yourself. You could have married Henry VIII."

"True." Liv laughed. "Why don't you two finish the tour without me? I'm not much in the mood, and I want to try Eli one more time. Since I've already made an utter sap of myself with all my other calls, what do I have to lose?"

"Are you sure?" Mel looked at her uncertainly, like she was torn between being there for her and finishing the tour with Pierce.

Liv waved her away. "Yes, of course. Even if Catherine's ghost follows me, I wager she'll be sympathetic to a fellow sufferer."

"Come on, then," Pierce said to Mel, and the minute he took Mel's hand, Liv could see her give in.

"Meet you in the gift shop, then," Liv said, heading

for the exit. She stepped outside into the crisp, overcast day and found a relatively comfortable spot on one of the benches in what was left of the now-frozen garden. But it was peaceful, and the icicles hanging from the trees and shrubs were lovely. She dialed Eli and had already so successfully prepped herself for another humbling message that she jumped when he picked up on the third ring.

"Eli?" she started haltingly. "It's me . . . Liv."

There was a brief pause, and then a quiet, "I know."

"I'm so glad I finally got you. Have you been getting my messages?"

"Yes," Eli said. "I just needed some time to think before we talked."

Liv gripped the phone and sat rigid on the bench, dreading what she knew was coming. He'd say he didn't fancy her anymore, that he didn't believe her story about Pierce just being a friend. And it would all be over. She closed her eyes against the ache that was already starting in her chest. How could she bear it?

"You say that Pierce is a friend," Eli started. "Fine. I believe it. And that the fake date was just to appease your mother. Okay. I'm willing to buy into that, too. At first, I was furious about the whole situation, but then I realized I wasn't really mad about the ridiculous date story."

"You weren't?" Liv said, her eyes flying open.

"No. I was angrier that you didn't defend our dating, or me, to your parents," he said. "I don't need their approval to make this relationship work. But the frustrating thing is . . . you do."

"That's not true," Liv said, her cheeks flushing at the accusation. "I'm perfectly capable of making my own decisions, with or without their consent."

Eli sighed. "I know that, babe. But then the question is . . . why don't you?"

Liv stared up at the gray sky. It was a good question . . . a bloody great question. The only problem was, she had no idea how to answer it.

"Look, I'm not mad anymore, not really. Just disappointed, but I'm working on getting over it. Since I don't want to lose you over this, you'll just have to put up with a few more days of my sulking. Okay?"

"Of course," Liv said, smiling in relief. "Save that thought."

Eli laughed. "I spent the last few days checking into flights, and I found a great deal. Roundtrip for a couple hundred. Even a starving cinematographer can afford that, and I've got the tickets on hold until midnight tonight. So what do you say?"

Liv struggled to suck in a breath, her lungs suddenly deflating. Everything in her shouted that she should be thrilled, but she could barely hear that over the deafening static of panic in her head. How could she even ask her parents for permission now, when they thought she'd finally opened up to the idea of dating Pierce? Even if she made up some excuse and said that she and Pierce weren't clicking, her mum would never agree to let Eli fly over. Especially now that her mum believed she'd been keeping the Florentina apprenticeship from her, too. Then again, wasn't Eli's whole point that she didn't have to ask permission for everything, that she needed to stand up to her parents to fight for what she truly wanted?

"Liv?" Eli said, pulling her out of her thoughts. "You still there?"

Liv finally found her voice, but it sounded mousy and pathetic, even to her. "I'm here. Eli, I . . ." She bit her lip, hating herself for what she was doing. "I don't know if a visit is such a good idea."

"For who?" Eli asked, a brisk, harder tone entering into his voice. "Your parents, or you?"

"My parents," Liv said meekly, "and me. Mum found out about the Florentina apprenticeship and she told Emily I wouldn't be taking it. I can't get her to listen to reason. Things are such a mess right now, and I just can't handle any more battles at the moment."

"I get it," Eli said, his voice rising. "If it's that big of a stress for you, then forget it. Forget the whole thing."

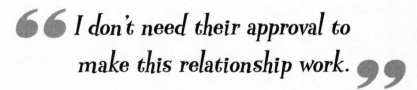

I don't need their approval to make this relationship work.

"What are you saying?" Liv whispered.

"I'm saying I don't know if this is going to work," Eli said. "It's obvious I'm not good enough for your parents, and you're not willing to fight for what you want. If this *is* what you want, which I'm not even sure about." The strain in his voice got stronger. "I should've figured this out a long time ago. Things aren't going to change between you and your parents. You'll always be caving to them, no matter what you have to sacrifice to do it."

"Eli." Her voice warbled as she fought tears. "I'm so sorry. I just don't think it's a good time. But I'll see you when I get back to New York. Things will be back to normal then."

"Normal would be a boyfriend getting to visit his girlfriend over the holidays, and meeting her parents, finally," Eli said. "Normal isn't using New York City as a hideout from your parents, and things you're afraid to deal with." He sighed. "I have to go. I'm turning in my film tomorrow to Professor Heffen, and I've still got at least five hours of editing ahead of me."

"I'll call you later this week, okay?" Liv said. "And I'll be back in town on Saturday. Maybe I'll see you this weekend before I fly back home again?"

She waited through the painful silence, her heart thundering in her ears.

"I don't know," Eli finally said quietly. "We'll see."

Liv just nodded, not able to speak anymore.

Somehow, she managed to get off the phone before the tears spilled over, but then she let them fall freely in warm rivers down her cheeks. She didn't know how much time passed before she finally pulled herself up from the bench, wiped her eyes, and went back inside. She caught up with Mel and Pierce as they finished the tour of the Queen's Chambers.

One look at Liv's face was all it took for Mel to give her a hug. "It didn't go well?"

"It went terribly," Liv said. "I think . . . I think we might be breaking up, and it's my sodding fault. I've screwed up everything."

"I'm sure that's not true," Mel said. "What happened?"

Liv shook her head. "I don't want to talk about it. I think I just want to go home."

"We'll go with you," Mel offered, and Pierce nodded.

"Yeah, we'll cancel the dinner cruise, no problem," he said.

"Not on my account, you won't," Liv said. "You shouldn't have to suffer through a night with a sad sack. You two go on and have fun. Giles can pick me up from here. Besides, I have to finish up my jewelry pieces for *Flirt* tonight. It'll be a good distraction."

Mel started to protest, but Liv refused to listen. "I might be a pushover with my parents, but I'm putting my foot down with you," she said, trying for a joke, but falling miserably short. "I'll be fine. I promise."

But after Liv said good-bye to them and Giles picked her up, fresh tears started falling all over again, and she knew she was far from fine, and she had only herself to blame for that.

⟡   ⟡   ⟡   ⟡

Liv had no idea how much time had passed when she heard the knock on her bedroom door. For once, since her mum was out running some errands for the ball, she'd had some time alone at home, and it had been such a relief not to face any questions about Pierce or Eli. She'd been working for hours, ever since she got back from Hampton Court, in an attempt to keep from obsessing over Eli. It hadn't really worked, but at least she'd kept busy.

"Come in," she said, and Mel poked her head around the door.

"In the mood for some company?" Mel asked.

"Sure," Liv said. "I'm just finishing up." She attached the clasp to the last choker she'd made for the Barney's display. She leaned back in her chair, stretched her sore muscles, and examined the dozen earring and necklace sets she'd finished. She'd designed each of them in a combination of Victorian and modern styles, and the result was an intertwining of delicate filigree pendants with geometrical shapes and sleek, hammered chains or collars.

"These are fab," Mel said as she carefully picked up one of the earrings and held it up to the light. "Your best yet. You keep going like this, and you'll have your own label in Tiffany someday."

"Such rubbish," Liv said, rolling her eyes, but she was secretly delighted with the compliment.

"Seriously, Liv, Demetria is going to love these," Mel said. "I've never seen anything like them. They're one-of-a-kind Olivia Bourne-Cecil."

Liv could only hope Mel was right, because her boss, the great fashion editrix Demetria Tish, was one tough critic. "It was hard working from just the photos of the outfits she e-mailed me," Liv said. "I'm not sure I got the colors right, and you know the outfits always look different on the mannequins than they do on the racks."

Mel waved her hand dismissively. "Let me tell you what's what," she said. "The minute the displays are unveiled, shoppers are going to be flocking to the Barney's jewelry counter asking for your masterpieces. So you better get busy making yourself some business cards, because the orders are going to come rolling in."

Liv sighed. "I don't think I'll be filling many orders under Mum's roof this Christmas, but thanks for the kudos." She made a concerted effort to snap herself out of the doom and gloom thoughts and smiled at Mel. "By the way, don't you have some dishing to do, of the date details variety? How did it go with Pierce?"

Mel grinned sheepishly. "The dinner cruise was so romantic. We talked and danced the entire time."

"Oh, and I think you did more than that," Liv teased. "Was it an all-out snogfest?"

Mel laughed. "Just a little snogging, but *very* delish. Enough to make me forget about Nick Lyric, anyway."

"Pierce and Lord Northam are coming to the ball on Friday," Liv said, "so no doubt you'll have more opportunities for snogging then."

"Not while your mom's around," Mel said, then giggled. "I never knew a clandestine romance could be so much fun."

Liv nodded. "Maybe that's what I should have tried with Eli, too. It might have been better if mum had never found out I was dating him."

Mel squeezed her hand. "Everything will work out. You'll see."

"I wish I could be certain of that," Liv said as another knock sounded on the door and her mum came in, carrying a garment bag.

"Hello, girls. I just came from the city, and I picked up a little something for you, Mel."

Liv nearly laughed at Mel's shocked expression when she asked, "For me?"

" *I can see you've come to your senses about the silliness with Eli.* **"**

Her mum nodded. "I know you were planning on borrowing something of Liv's for the ball, but you're taller than she is, and I thought this might suit you better." She unzipped the bag and carefully pulled out a sleek black chiffon gown with an elegant cranberry sash that fell from the nape of the neck down the back into a short, fanlike train. "It's on loan from Vivienne Westwood's until Saturday."

"It's gorgeous," Mel whispered, running her hands over the filmy, pillowy-soft fabric. "Thank you so much."

"Well, you were very helpful with the exhibit brochure," Liv's mum said, "so it was the least I could do." She left the garment bag on the back of Liv's armchair and turned to go, then stopped briefly to glance at Liv's handiwork. Liv held her breath, waiting for her mum's reaction.

"I'm sure Josephine will appreciate the time you've put into these, Olivia," she said. "They're quite unique, although a little too contemporary for my tastes. But I'm glad you're spending your time productively. I can see you've come to your senses about the Florentina apprenticeship and forgotten all about this silliness with Eli. And rightly so."

"Yes, Mum," Liv barely managed to whisper, fighting fresh tears.

"Good night," her mum said, kissing her lightly on the cheek before sweeping out of the room.

"Oh, Liv, I'm sorry," Mel said. "She should have stopped at 'hello.'"

Liv wiped her eyes and starting putting her jewelry away, all except one piece she was going to wear to the ball on Friday. "Well," she said, "she's treating you better now. That's at least something." But she knew in her heart it wasn't nearly enough.

ⓖ   ⓖ   ⓖ   ⓖ

FLIRT-SPACE

Posted by <u>ChicaSnappa</u> Wednesday 5:42 P.M.

The good (and the highlight of the last week): I met Bjorn V and got a contract offer from him.

The bad: I failed my math midterm, ditched work last night, and was told in no uncertain terms by *mis padres* that I will never be a model. *Adios*, Bjorn!

The ugly: I got the rest of my midterm grades today. *Oye*. Am I in some hot water now! I may be spending the rest of my life in perpetual summer school in Argentina under lock and key. Farewell, *mis amigas*.

Sightings: Mother Michael's vein pulsating on her forehead when she handed me my midterm grades this afternoon; purgatorial flames shooting out of Lynn's eyes when I turned in my prints for the holiday issue late and then tried to apologize for skipping out on work yesterday afternoon; the cowhide couches in Ms. Bishop's office twice in the last four hours when I apologized (twice) for skipping work; Kiyoko's cold shoulder (seen repeatedly since my *muy estupido* argument with her).

Comments (1)

WriterGrrl **said:** Lexa, take some deep calming breaths, girlfriend! We'll be back in three days and we'll figure everything out then. If your parents come to take you into custody between now and then . . . RUN! Because you are NOT going back to Argentina.

chapter twelve

Kiyoko leaned back in Belle's chair and took in the incredible view of the cityscape from the floor-to-ceiling windows. She could so get used to this. Belle had no idea, but she was ruining the cube farm for Kiyoko forever more. Since Belle had entrusted her with finishing the Basil Shade exclusive in the privacy of her office, Kiyoko had had the prime VIP seat in here for the last four days. Sure, she'd drained midtown of nearly all its caffeine supply rewriting and revising her article, and she was eating, sleeping, and dreaming Basil's "Silent Night" by this point, but getting to play Entertainment editor from Belle's chair had made it all worth it.

She clicked a photo of the view with her Razr phone and texted Cody:

> **KIYoKO!!!: Check out the view from my fab new office. I'm moving up, boyo!**
> **DJCody: U squatter, u! Keep dreaming, Kiyoko! U keep landing exclusives like Basil's and you might get there.**
> **KIYoKO!!!: U know it.**

"I see you're hard at work," a voice said, and Kiyoko snapped to attention to see Belle leaning over her shoulder to peer at her computer screen, where the cursor had been blinking in the same exact place for the last ten minutes. Somehow, Belle had stealthily swept into the room without Kiyoko noticing.

"Forgive me, my liege," Kiyoko said. "I was just giving my taxed brain cells a brief reprieve."

Belle's lips hinted at a smile, but it slipped away as she said, "The reprieve will have to wait until tomorrow, anime girl. Ms. Bishop isn't exactly thrilled that I've excused you from working with the other interns on the displays at Barney's this afternoon, and she wants to see our product for the issue by five today."

"It's all under control," Kiyoko said swiftly, wanting to reassure her. She'd noticed that the normally calm and collected Belle was bordering on high strung this week, spending most of the time with her office door closed, except when Kiyoko was in there working. "I'm just finishing up the rewrite on the last paragraph, and then all I need to do is proofread it and stream the digital music files onto the network so we can pick them up for the website."

"Good," Belle said, grabbing her Coach bag and coat. "I've got to run to a meeting downtown. Just leave a clean printout on my desk and save the article onto my memory stick. But leave the music files on a CD here. I'll stream them in later. I want to check them one more time beforehand."

Kiyoko saluted. "Consider it done." Then she paused. "Belle, do you think Ms. Bishop's going to like it?"

"I'd say yes, but I never promise anyone accolades, not in this industry," Belle said. "It's my job to explore the fringe, whether she likes it or not. Got it?"

Kiyoko nodded, but an uneasy feeling settled over her after Belle left. This was all a little too under-the-table for her taste. Normally she was all about pushing the envelope, but was Belle going too far with this? Kiyoko had sat in on several meetings in the last week where Ms. Bishop had reiterated the importance of reaffirming their presence in fashion publishing, especially with *Élan* getting ready to launch their premiere issue. Maybe this wasn't the time for taking risks. But then again, maybe she was just getting cold feet for the first time in her life. Was it possible? Was she losing her edge? No. It wasn't possible. She set trends; she didn't follow them.

She settled back into her work, and in no time at all had her edits finished. She smiled proudly as she printed the document. It was good. No, it was great. She was just about to save her masterpiece to Belle's memory stick when an e-mail blipped up onto Belle's screen. Kiyoko went to close it, but then the subject line caught her eye: "Basil Shade exclusive."

Wait a sec. No one else at *Flirt* knew about this except her and Belle, did they? Oh, and Lexa, but she'd never spill anything. Kiyoko glanced at the e-mail addie and sucked in her breath. The e-mail was from someone at *Élan* magazine! Those sneaks! How did they know anything about the exclusive? Now she *had* to see what this e-mail was all about.

From: vivian_c@elan.com
To: belle_h@flirt.com
Re: Basil Shade exclusive

Ms. Holder,
Per our agreement, we are expecting your exclusive first thing tomorrow morning. I'm assuming you're still interested in the editor-in-chief position here, and once we have the article, you can consider yourself hired. We look forward to a very long and lucrative relationship with you.

Best,
Vivian Cavaneux
VP and Publisher, *Élan* Magazine

Oh. My. Nondenominational. God. Belle, her beloved insurgent of a boss, had turned to the Dark Side! Kiyoko stared at the e-mail, trying to wish it away. No wonder Belle had been so careful about keeping this project hush-hush. When she figured Ms. Bishop would never go for it, she must have gotten fed up enough to go to *Élan* with the idea. Belle was constantly battling Ms. Bishop and Trey to push for edgier product, sure, but to sell her soul to the competition? That was traitorous, not trend-breaking.

Kiyoko numbly grabbed her memory stick, the hard copy of the article, and the music files and dumped them into her bag, then closed Belle's e-mail and frantically scrambled to leave the office, which suddenly gave her a feeling of contamination. This was so far out of her league, she needed some reinforcements. And as much as she hated to admit it, there was only one person she could think of who she could trust with this mammoth crisis. The one person she'd been avoiding all week, but who she needed to talk to more than anything right now.

ⓖ　　ⓖ　　ⓖ　　ⓖ

She found Alexa hard at work behind the curtained glass of the Barney's window displays, papering the back wall with a photo collage from the "Naughty and Nice" shoot. Gen was dressing mannequins in the outfits from the shoot, and Charlotte was setting up a Christmas tree decorated with Fendi, Ferragamo, and Manolo Blahnik shoes, hung like ornaments from its branches.

"Well, look who finally decided to join us," Gen said, glowering, "and what perfect timing, too. We're just finishing up for today."

"Drama queen, much, Gen?" Kiyoko asked. "It must be tough being the *Flirt* martyr, but hey, somebody's go to do it." She smiled as Gen huffily turned back to the mannequin she was working on, yanking a Caroline Herrera gown over its head like it was a Kmart special.

Then she turned to Alexa, who hadn't said a word since she'd shown up. She looked like she hadn't slept in a week, which, Kiyoko realized, she probably hadn't. Her normally luminous thick hair was tied haphazardly back in a scarf and her eyes were red and glassy from exhaustion. Kiyoko had seen her upset before, but not anywhere near this, and suddenly a lot of the anger she'd felt toward Alexa over the last few days washed away in worry for her friend.

"Lexa," she said. "Can I talk to you for a sec? Alone?"

Nothing. Not even so much as shake of her head. When Alexa didn't move from the spot, Kiyoko tried again, stepping closer to whisper. "Blimey, lad, I'm sorry it's been a hard week for you, but you can't blame me for being peeved at you lately with all the no-shows and IOUs you've pulled."

Alexa paused and stepped down from her ladder. "I'm sorry for that, Kiko," she said, "and for going off on you at MoMA the other day. I was the one who messed up everything with school and Bjorn V. I shouldn't have taken it out on you. I just don't know what's going to happen with anything anymore."

Kiyoko nodded. "I hear that, but in the meantime, I'm here for you, no matter what happens. And so are Mel and Liv . . . in spirit, anyway. And believe it or not, Kiko-cita needs your advice."

Alexa gave a short laugh. "*Chiquita*, I don't think so. Just take a look at *mi vida loca*. I'm the last person who should be giving advice."

"But you're the only person I can trust with this, mate," Kiyoko said seriously. "It's about Belle and the Basil Shade exclusive." This time Alexa gave her a questioning look, then nodded.

"*Ven conmigo,*" she said, motioning for Kiyoko to follow her. Once they were safely out of Gen and Charlotte's hearing range, she said. "*Digame*. Tell me everything."

෬ ෬ ෬ ෬

This was it. It was going to be *sayonara Flirt*, Kiyoko was sure of it. How had Alexa managed to convince her to go to Ms. Bishop and Trey with the whole story? And what had she been thinking when she agreed? This was all one horrible, nightmarish mistake.

She chanced a sideways glance at Alexa, who was sitting beside her on the cowhide couch in Ms. Bishop's stark white office, and was slightly calmed to see Alexa give her an encouraging nod. She was so glad Alexa had agreed to come with her to explain everything to Ms. Bishop. Having her there made it all easier to handle. But then she looked at Trey's furrowed brow and Ms. Bishop's face of impenetrable steel as they finished reading Belle's e-mail from *Élan*, and her momentary calm crumbled into panic.

Her Lordship rarely let her composure fail, and Kiyoko was sure this meant one thing: absolute and total annihilation. The only question was, who was her unlucky target?

Finally, Ms. Bishop looked up from the e-mail. "Well, Ms. Katsuda," she started, "you've taken an incredible risk coming to me with such a strong accusation. You've violated several of our corporate policies regarding privacy in the workplace, not to mention acted in direct opposition to orders from your immediate supervisor."

"Yes," Kiyoko acknowledged, willing her eyes not to drop from Ms. Bishop's. "I know the rules, but in this case, with the best interests of *Flirt* in mind, I thought they should be broken."

"I see," Ms. Bishop said. "So some of Belle *has* rubbed off on you, then. Her irreverence for rules has made her name in this industry, and I see a similar vein running through you, too. Just take care that, unlike her, you continue to use sound judgment to determine when it's appropriate to bend and break them." Her nails tapped loudly on her desk with the sound of a gavel handing down a sentence. "In this case, I'm grateful for your act of indiscretion. It would have been unfortunate to be outshone by our competitor."

"What will happen to the exclusive?" Kiyoko asked. "Basil's going to be immense once his contract goes public. We can't just trash the article, not when it could bring EBM and Basil into the mainstream." Kiyoko stopped, cursing herself for opening her mouth.

But instead of chastising her, Ms. Bishop asked simply, "You truly believe Basil is going to break out with this new album?"

"Absolutely," Kiyoko said firmly. "It's the bomb."

"He does have a unique sound," Trey acknowledged. "And his substantial underground following could end up being a new set of avid readers for us."

Ms. Bishop nodded thoughtfully, then flipped through the article one last time. "We'll run your exclusive on Basil in our next issue under your name. And now, if you'll excuse us, Trey and I have some important decisions to make regarding this incident that do not concern either of you ladies. Why don't you go home? Ms. Veron, I'll explain to Lynn why you've left. Belle will be coming back to the office shortly, and I'd prefer to speak to her without involving either of you."

"*Arigato gozaimashita,*" Kiyoko said, standing up with Alexa to leave. "Thank you."

"Thank you, Kiyoko," Trey said.

Outside the office, Alexa collapsed against the wall. "*Dios mio*, I've had way too many run-ins with Ms. Bishop in the last two weeks. It's just not healthy."

Kiyoko grinned in relief. "Well, at least this time, you weren't the one in front of the firing squad."

"*Es verdad*, but my trial by fire isn't over yet, either."

Kiyoko nodded, suddenly feeling a pang at the thought of how lonely the Flirt-cave would be if Alexa got sent back to Argentina. And the jury was still out on that account. "Lexa, thanks for coming with me tonight," she said. "I couldn't have done it without you."

"*No problema, chiquita*. It was the least I could do after walking around with *mi cabeza* in my caboose for the last two weeks." She stepped toward the elevators. "Come on. Emma promised me some homemade knishes tonight to help take my mind off *mis padres* and my grades. She said if I'm going to go home for good soon, the least she can do is give me a true Manhattan send-off."

"Hold the elevator for me, lad," Kiyoko said, coming to a split-second decision about something she'd been debating for most of the last half hour with Ms. Bishop. "I forgot something in Ms. Bishop's office. I'll be right there."

"Is there something else, Ms. Katsuda?" Ms. Bishop said when she waved her back in.

Kiyoko took a deep breath. "I was just wondering if you might talk to Alexa's parents and principal about her modeling contract with Bjorn V," she said. "It means so much to her, and I know she can pull her grades up if she's given a chance."

"Unfortunately, Ms. Veron is dangerously close to losing more than her modeling contract at the moment," Ms. Bishop said. "It's up to her parents, her teachers, and me to decide what's best for her right now. And sometimes even when a seemingly great opportunity presents itself, it's not always the best course of action to take."

"I understand," Kiyoko said. "But if you could just think about it . . ."

Ms. Bishop held her eyes for a long moment, then finally nodded. "We'll see."

Kiyoko thanked her and ran to catch the elevator. She'd done what she could, and now it was all out of her hands. But she hoped, for Alexa's sake, that there was still a chance to make everything right.

ᓂ   ᓂ   ᓂ   ᓂ

Kiyoko was just finishing her second helping of potato knishes and stretching out on the couch with Alexa to watch the episode of *Lost* she'd saved on TiVO, when Gen and Charlotte burst into the loft in a flurry of chatter.

"Well, Kiyoko, as of tomorrow," Gen said

triumphantly as she hung up her coat, "your boss is history."

"¿Qué paso?" Alexa said, sending a "Let's play stupid" signal to Kiyoko with her eyes. "We left the office right at five."

"No one knows for sure what the sitch was," Charlotte said, "but a memo went out after hours tonight via e-mail, saying that Belle Holder was no longer employed by *Flirt*."

"Harsh," Kiyoko muttered. She'd guessed as much when they'd left the *Flirt* office earlier, but still, she felt a twinge of sadness at the thought of not having Belle around to stir things up. She'd been a great boss, right up until her ego got the better of her.

"She was escorted out of the building right as we were coming in to get our things after Barney's," Gen said. "I told you Aunt Josephine was getting tired of dealing with her. She was such an agitator, and they never last."

"Oh, but sometimes they do, Genevieve," a cool voice said from the doorway.

Kiyoko gave a brief snort of laughter into the couch pillows as Gen turned shades paler at the sight of Ms. Bishop standing in the entryway.

"I didn't climb the rungs of *Flirt* with a safety harness on," Ms. Bishop said, keeping her piercing gaze on Gen. "There are times when catalysts are a necessity for positive change."

"Of course, Aunt Josephine—I mean, Ms. Bishop," Gen stammered. "You're right."

Ms. Bishop glossed over Gen's brown-nosing and looked at Alexa. "Ms. Veron, may I speak to you for a moment alone?"

"Of course," Alexa said, leaping òff the couch and leading the way into her bedroom, where Ms. Bishop quietly shut the door behind them.

For Kiyoko, the next five minutes were torturous, but when Alexa finally reemerged with Ms. Bishop, there it was: a genuine, stress-free smile on Alexa's face, the first of its kind Kiyoko had seen in weeks. As soon as Ms. Bishop left, Alexa did a jubilant dance around the living room, snapping her hands like castanets.

"All right, who's stampeding like elephants in here?" Emma said, popping her head into the flat. But when she saw Alexa doing a meringue, she smiled.

"I'm staying!" Alexa sang. "I'm staying!"

"Yes! I knew it, mate!" Kiyoko rolled off the couch and started dancing, too.

"That's great, Alexa." Emma beamed, giving her a hug. "It wouldn't have been the same around here without you."

"Ms. Bishop confabbed with *mis padres* and Mother Michael tonight," Alexa said gleefully. "She convinced them that the modeling contract would be good for my résumé and my photography. I can take it under two conditions.

I get a tutor on the weekends to bring up my grades, and go to summer school to make up my math grade. And I live in the dorms at St. Catherine's next summer while I work with Bjorn, so that Mother Michael can keep an eye on me." She rolled her eyes, but she was laughing as she did. "Mother Michael has *nada* idea what she's in for. In Argentina, my specialty was dorm pranks."

"Poor Mother Michael." Kiyoko laughed. "I hope she doesn't have a weak heart."

"Just remember how short-lived a modeling career can be, Alexa," Gen said huffily. "That's part of the reason I've decided not to actively pursue a contract, even though I've had plenty of offers."

"As you've told us," Kiyoko said with a hint of sarcasm, "many times. Funny how we've never actually seen you in any photo shoots, though." That shut Gen up, and Kiyoko took the opportunity to grab all of their coats. "Come on, lads, this calls for a celebration. I hear the SoHo Cupcake Company calling."

"Knishes *and* cupcakes?" Emma cried, laughing. "I can feel the heartburn already."

Kiyoko smiled at Alexa's glowing face as they headed for the door, glad that she'd finally caught a break. And in just two more days, Liv and Mel would be back for an even bigger celebration. She couldn't wait.

chapter thirteen

Mel had thought galas in New York were impressive, but that was before she saw the glitz at the Tate ball on Friday night. She could honestly say that even though Mrs. B-C was seriously high-strung, she knew how to throw one fab party. Of course, Mel and Liv had spent most of Friday helping with the final preparations, but Mrs. B-C was the ultimate hostess.

Mel had watched her move deftly around the room, greeting the guests with grace for the past two hours. Mrs. B-C hadn't even blinked when Gwyneth and Chris had walked in, or when the Duke of Westminster had offhandedly purchased three of Maia's paintings for his estate, apparently without any regard for the six-figure price tags. It amazed Mel even more that this was the world Liv had grown up in, and the one she'd return to once her time at *Flirt* was over. Everywhere Mel looked she saw London's finest wearing the season's latest formal fashions, draped in expensive-looking jewelry while they sipped Cristal champagne and admired Maia Cardinale's artwork.

"Would you like a glass, Mel?" Pierce asked beside her, following her eyes to the waiter walking by with gold-flecked flutes.

"Is it on par with Almas caviar?" Mel teased. "Because if that's the case, I'm not worthy."

Pierce gave her hand a brief squeeze, careful to make sure no one but Liv noticed. "In that dress, Mel, the question is whether the champagne is worthy of you."

"Quite right, Pierce," Liv said. "She looks completely gorge."

Mel smiled, a thrill running through her where Pierce's hand had been. She could so get used to this. And of course, now she was leaving tomorrow morning. Just her luck. But she was certainly enjoying it while it lasted. She just wished she and Pierce didn't have to be so careful around Mrs. B-C, but then again, she didn't want Liv to have to fess up to Mrs. B-C either, especially since she still hadn't been able to get ahold of Eli. The easier things were for Liv tonight, the better.

"What do you say, Liv?" Mel asked. "A little bubbly on our last night in London?"

"I thought you'd never ask," Liv said jokingly.

"Then allow me," Pierce said gallantly, giving a half bow that made both girls giggle. But when he got a few feet away, he was swept up by Lord Northam for some introductions.

"Hmm," Liv said. "Looks like it might take awhile."

"Uh-oh," Mel said, nodding over Liv's shoulder to Mrs. B-C leading a middle-aged woman in a black velvet gown trimmed with cream lace their way. "Don't look now, but I think we're about to come under attack, too."

Liv followed Mel's eyes, then whispered. "It's Victoria Billingsley, the Countess of Essex. She's one of Mum's best clients, and one of the wealthiest aristocrats in England."

Before Mel could respond, Mrs. B-C and the countess had descended upon them. The countess made a big show making Euro kisses to Liv and demurely offering her hand to Mel as Mrs. B-C introduced her.

"Olivia, I haven't been able to take my eyes off of this all evening." She delicately ran her hand over Liv's choker. "Wherever did you find such a stunning piece?"

Liv blushed. "Actually, I made it. I make jewelry in my spare time."

"She just dabbles in it, really," Mrs. B-C explained. "It's one of her hobbies."

"Hobbies, for shame," the countess repeated, clucking her tongue. "Look at that handiwork. It should be much more than a hobby." She opened her bag and retrieved her pocketbook, all business. "Now, I will gladly pay you in advance for one of your ensembles, and I'd like to place an order right now."

Liv smiled. "Thank you so much," she said,

66 *Don't look now, but I think we're about to come under attack, too.* 99

beaming. "It would be an honor to create something for you."

They worked through the details of payment and design. Mel grinned and nearly giggled when she saw a look of astonishment pass fleetingly across Mrs. B-C's face before she had the chance to compose herself.

"My dear," the countess said, leaning conspiratorially toward Liv, "I have at least two dozen friends who would kill for something this divine. And a Bourne-Cecil original, too. You and your mother are so much alike. You both have an exquisite eye for masterpieces. Where did you receive your training in jewelry design?"

"I'm self-taught, really," Liv said shyly. "But I've been working on some pieces for *Flirt* magazine, and . . ." she hesitated, glancing at her mother, then took a deep breath. "And I've been offered an apprenticeship at Florentina in New York for the summer that I'm considering." This time, Liv looked pointedly at her mother, who remained coolly unfazed, at least on the exterior. "It would be a wonderful chance to learn more about design. And then after that, I plan to take out a small business loan to open a flagship boutique here in London. I can run it while I attend university."

Mel stared at Liv, not believing what she was hearing. She was witnessing a mutiny, right here. Quiet, people-pleasing Liv was finally taking a stand! She must have known that Mrs. B-C would never dare argue with her in front of her colleagues. Now Liv clearly had the countess's undivided attention, and—an even bigger surprise—her mother's, too.

"What a marvelous opportunity at Florentina," the countess gushed. "You can hone your business sense while you set up shop." Then, she added to Mrs. B-C, "Eleanor, I never knew your daughter had such talent and common sense. You must let my personal realtor help her scout out the perfect location for the boutique."

"Well, I . . . I hadn't really given it much thought . . ." Mrs. B-C stuttered, but the countess ignored her and turned to Liv. "What will you call the shop, dear?"

"Divinations," Liv said with such unfailing certainty that Mel knew she must have had that name picked out from the moment she'd designed her first piece.

"Glorious," the countess said. "Here's my direct line and my realtor's card. Be sure to contact her right away."

"Of course," Liv said. "Thank you so much."

"Not at all. Now, if you'll kindly excuse me, I must go say hello to Lord Collins."

She glided away in a flourish of velvet and lace, leaving Mrs. B-C staring after her, dumbfounded.

"Omigod, Liv!" Mel hugged Liv. "Your jewelry's found favor with royalty! That's what I call moving on up."

Liv laughed, then looked her mother straight in the eye. "Well, Mum, what do you think now? Are you willing to admit that I might have some inkling of what I'm doing?"

Mrs. B-C looked at her long and hard. Then, she cleared her throat. "Perhaps your designs do show some potential after all," she admitted. "And . . . maybe exploring the possibility of a boutique could help open your eyes to the challenges of running your own business. As long as your schoolwork takes precedence, of course."

"Of course," Liv said. "And what about the Florentina apprenticeship? All I'm asking for is one more summer."

Mel held her breath as she watched Mrs. B-C struggle with the decision. And for Liv's sake, she hoped for the impossible.

"I suppose if an apprenticeship with Florentina is going to garner praise from the likes of the Countess of Essex, then I can't exactly refuse," she finally said. "And, if it means that much to you, I'll sign your paperwork first thing tomorrow and e-mail Emily Blanchette with my permission."

"And . . . maybe exploring the possibility of a boutique could help open your eyes to the challenges of running your own business. As long as your school-work takes precedence, of course."

"Thanks, Mum!" Liv said, her cheeks glowing with happiness.

Just then Mrs. B-C's cell rang, and she hushed Liv as she answered. "Oh, hello, Josephine," she sing-songed. "How lovely of you to ring . . ." She stepped away to finish the conversation, and Mel took the opportunity to give Liv a congratulatory hug.

"You are incredible!" she cried. "I didn't know you had it in you."

Liv shrugged. "I didn't know, either, but I'm well and fed up with tiptoeing around Mum's wishes. It's about time I did something about it."

Mel smiled. "I think this is the beginning of a whole new Liv. Before you know it, I'll have you wearing Birkenstocks and organic clothing."

"Never." Liv laughed. "You know I'd be lost without Hermès and Burberry."

"Melanie," Mrs. B-C suddenly called out, snapping her phone shut with authority, "did you happen to send Josephine Bishop a copy of your commentary on Maia's art?"

Oh no. Mel cringed. *That did not sound good.*

"Guilty as charged," she said hesitantly, trying to read Mrs. B-C's solemn face. "I sent it to her when I turned in my British fashion feature. I thought she might want to include an excerpt in the international section of the next issue."

"*Before you know it, I'll have you wearing Birkenstocks and organic clothing.*"

"Well, she doesn't," Mrs. B-C said soberly, then she smiled. "She wants to post the entire commentary on *Flirt*'s website instead! She says that Maia's palette is the perfect compliment to the colors in the 'Naughty and Nice' issue, and she'd love for you two to bring back one of the pieces to display at Barney's."

"That's brill, Mum," Liv said.

"What wonderful exposure for Maia," Mrs. B-C said, "and I have you to thank for it, Mel."

"I was just hoping to help." Mel shrugged nonchalantly, but she was secretly reveling in Mrs. B-C's gratitude. She'd finally won over the Wicked Witch of Hampstead Heath.

"I'm afraid I misjudged you," Mrs. B-C said, "and for that, I'm truly sorry. You know you're always welcome in our home, so we hope to see you back visiting us again soon."

"I'd like that," Mel said sincerely. Now that she'd passed the great Bourne-Cecil inquisition, she might actually enjoy another visit to Coventry Manor.

Then Mrs. B-C added with a knowing smile, "And I think, perhaps, there's a certain young man who would be happy to see you make another trip to London in the near future, too." She nodded toward Pierce, who had finally managed to get two champagne flutes, but was now cornered by Lord and Lady Ashford.

Mel blushed, completely speechless, but Liv cried, horrified, "Mum! How did you—"

"Oh, please, Olivia," Mrs. B-C said dismissively. "I may have hoped for a different match to come of this week's visit, but obviously you've had your heart set on someone else. And Pierce, I think, has, too." She laughed at Liv's shocked face. "I am not that blind, dear."

"In that case," Liv said, taking a deep breath, "there's something I wanted to ask you. I know you're not keen on Eli, but you've yet to meet him. I'd like you to give him a fair chance. And . . . I'd like to invite him to visit over the holidays."

"My, my, you *are* full of surprises this evening," Mrs. B-C said. "But you've certainly proven yourself to be a sound judge of character with Melanie, so I'll hope you've done the same with Eli." She sighed. "And I'll see for myself when he comes to visit."

"Thank you," Liv said, "for trusting me enough to agree to that."

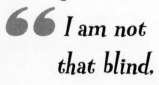
I am not that blind, dear.

Mrs. B-C nodded. "I suppose it's time I started."

"Cheers to that," Mel blurted out, forgetting for a second who she was talking to. But instead of getting angry, Mrs. B-C actually laughed.

"With such vocal opinions, Melanie, you'll make quite the essayist someday," she said just as Pierce finally appeared, triumphant, with the champagne. "Well, girls, I have guests to attend to. Giles will take you wherever you'd like to go after the ball, so enjoy your last night on the town."

"We will," Mel said as she left, then turned to Liv and Pierce. "So, where should we go to celebrate your emancipation?"

"I know a place," Liv said. "But we can't celebrate. Not yet. I have a phone call to make first."

◉   ◉   ◉   ◉

"How do you think it's going?" Pierce asked, motioning to where Liv was standing in the far corner of Ascot Lounge, talking on her cell.

"Hard to tell," Mel said, "but she's been on the phone for fifteen minutes and Eli hasn't hung up on her yet. I'm taking that as a good omen."

Pierce nodded. "I hope it all works out for them. I'd hate to lose my pseudo-girlfriend to anyone but a truly stellar chap."

Mel laughed. "Eli's great. And I hope you won't be too heartbroken."

Pierce grinned and slipped his hand over hers. "Somehow, I think I'll survive. In fact, I think I'm already interested in someone else. A literary type who's an ace fox-hunting saboteur with very beautiful eyes. But . . ." He sighed melodramatically. "She lives in the States."

"Hmmm. Well, the long distance thing *is* a problem," Mel said. "But you could always go visit her. If you wanted to, that is."

"True," Pierce said. "My father's planning a trip to New York in February, and he's offered to bring me along. I'm just not sure this girl's going to want to see me."

"I'm no expert," Mel said, "but I'm going to guess that she'd love to see you."

"Brilliant," Pierce said, flashing his heart-stopping smile. "And how do you think she'd feel about a send-off kiss?" he asked, brushing his hand across her cheek.

Mel's breath caught in her throat. "There's only one way to tell," she said, and leaning toward him, she touched her lips sweetly to his. "Very nice," she whispered as they pulled apart.

"All right, you two, no fair snogging in front of me when I'm six thousand miles away from my boyfriend," Liv called out, walking over to them with a wide smile. "You'll make a girl bloody jealous."

"So everything's okay with Eli?" Mel asked.

Liv nodded. "It took about a dozen apologies, but everything's fine. He's coming to the unveiling at Barney's

> **All right, you two, no fair snogging in front of me when I'm six thousand miles away from my boyfriend.**

with us tomorrow. And . . . he's booking his flight to Heathrow as we speak."

Mel hugged Liv. "I'm so glad it all worked out." She raised her glass of champagne. "*Now* can we celebrate?"

"Absolutely," Liv said.

Pierce raised his own glass in a toast. "To Liv's emancipation," he said. "And Mel, to your first trip to London, but hopefully not your last."

"*Definitely* not my last," Mel said, smiling as she clinked her glass to theirs. She'd be back someday. She was sure of it.

FLIRT-SPACE

Posted by <u>WriterGrrl</u> Friday 11:58 P.M.

Lexa and Keeks,

Liv and I got your e-mails tonight when we got back to the manor. We're so glad it all worked out, Lexa! I told you there was no way you'd be going back to Argentina. And Keeks, you have to fill us in on what happened with Belle when we get back tomorrow. We leave for two weeks, and there's a massive insurrection. Unbelievable! Can't wait to see you both tomorrow!

chapter fourteen

"**W**ake up!" two insanely cheerful voices cried into Alexa's darkened bedroom. "The British are coming! The British are coming!"

Alexa lifted her head blearily off the pillow as, amidst a mass of giggles, Liv and Mel tumbled into the room and flipped on the overhead light.

"*Oye,*" Alexa grumbled theatrically, trying to sound ferocious while hiding her growing smile under the sheets. Liv and Mel were back! *Finalmente!* "Haven't you ever heard of knocking?"

"Or how about my do-not-disturb until ten A.M. rule? I was up talking to Cody until the wee hours, and I need my sleep," Kiyoko griped, looking genuinely perturbed, or at least putting on a good show.

"You know you love us, Keeks," Mel said, plopping herself down on Kiyoko's bed.

For once Kiyoko couldn't deny it, but instead, she played the poor-me card one more time by pulling the sheets over her head. "What inhuman time of day is it, anyway?"

"Eight o'clock," Liv said. "We landed at JFK an hour ago.

We were going to wait to wake you, but then we decided we couldn't waste a minute of our last weekend together before the holidays."

"Besides, Keeks," Mel said, "I know you're *dying* to open your present."

One eye peeked through the blanket. "Present?"

Alexa laughed, leaping out of bed and rolling on top of Kiyoko. "*Andale, chiquita!* Get up already. I want *my* present *pronto*."

"All right, lads," came the muffled reply. "But someone go get me some coffee before I commit hari-kari. *Please*."

"Already thought of that," Mel said, handing her a gingerbread latte and a package wrapped in Harrod's paper.

Alexa got her fave from Liv—a double espresso mocha—and a package, too.

Kiyoko quickly gulped a sizable portion of the coffee, and then she and Alexa ripped open their packages.

"*Dios mio!*" Alex cried, cradling an antique tin-type camera in her arms. "Where did you find it?"

"At an antique store in Cecil Court," Mel said. "You like?"

"*Lo quiero,*" Alexa said, hugging Liv and Mel. "I love."

They all looked at Kiyoko, who had finally broken down and cracked a smile at her gifts—a Hello Kitty doll in a Beefeater outfit and half a dozen Brit underground CDs. "Roll Deep, Raghav, and Sway Dasafo," Kiyoko said, flipping through the CDs. "Choice, lads. Liv, for someone who's been known to hum 'Breakaway,' your taste in underground is impressive."

"Cheeky," Liv said. "But I can't take the credit. Mel picked most of them out."

Mel shrugged. "I've overheard your playlists blaring from your laptop for the last four months, Keeks. Osmosis."

Kiyoko popped one of the CDs into her stereo and Roll Deep blasted through the room for all of about ten seconds before Gen burst through the door in all her early-morning glory, complete with iridescent blue hydrating overnight facial mask.

"Do you mind?" she shrieked over the music, stomping over to turn it off. "Some people are trying to sleep so that they can be at their best for the Barney's unveiling this afternoon."

"I'm not sure the face mask is going to help with that," Alexa whispered to Liv, who barely managed to turn her giggle into a polite cough.

66 *I've overheard your playlists blaring from your laptop for the last four months, Keeks. Osmosis.* 99

"No prob, Gen," Mel said in her typical good-natured fashion. "We'll be out of your hair in a few." She pulled out a bag of Green and Blacks chocolate and handed it to Gen. "We picked this up for you and Charlotte."

"Um," Gen mumbled, clearly flustered by the act of kindness. "Thanks." She quietly left the room, and the girls broke into muffled laughter.

"Well, we better get going," Mel said to Liv, and Liv nodded.

"Where?" Alexa asked.

Mel nodded. "Liv and I made reservations at Balthazar for brunch. We called from the cab on the way here. Liv and I have to head uptown to drop off a painting at Barney's for the display after we eat, so can you guys be ready in fifteen?"

"For eggs bella donna at Balthazar?" Alexa said. "*Por supuesto*. I'll be ready in ten."

After Mel and Liv said a quick hi to Emma, the four girls walked the few blocks to Balthazar through a light, misty snowfall. Over café au laits and steaming plates of eggs and fresh pastries, they caught up with one another on everything that had happened over the last two weeks. Alexa filled Liv and Mel in on her mini-drama with Mother Michael and her parents and then told them her contract plans with Bjorn V. Kiyoko told all about Belle and the Basil exclusive, and Liv and Mel gave a day-by-day account of their time in London.

"I'm going to need help scouting out places for Divinations in London this spring," Liv said, "so I thought maybe all four of us could go next time."

"*Ciertamente,*" Alexa said, thrilled with the idea. "I'm there."

"Me too," Kiyoko said. "I'm dying to meet Mel's British boy-toy. Nick, schmick."

Mel blushed. "You might get to meet him before then. He could be coming here in February." She shrugged. "Whatever happens, happens. And in the meantime, I have the memory of my fling with the charming aristocrat to keep me going. And I'm going to be busy writing in my free time, too."

"The Great American Granola Novel?" Kiyoko asked.

Mel shook her head and smiled shyly. "Actually, I've been working on something for a while. I didn't want to say anything about it until I was finished, but . . . it's a series of essays about us."

"*Qué?*" Alexa asked.

"About the four of us together in New York," Mel said. "What we've done, what we've seen. You know, Liv meeting Eli and waitressing at Moe's, Kiyoko landing her music deal with Matsumoto, me getting stuck on the subway on our first night out in the city and ending up in Brooklyn.

" The Great American Granola Novel? "

> **If our stories are going to be in print, lads, we better make sure every second of the rest of our time here counts.**

And you," she added, grinning at Alexa, "you chasing down celebs with your camera."

"Cool," Kiyoko said. "The *Flirt* four do Manhattan. It could work."

"That's brilliant, Mel," Liv said. "Are you going to try to get it published when you're done?"

"Maybe," Mel said. "I'm editing it now, and then I'm going to leave a copy with Ms. Bishop to read over the holidays."

Alexa let out a low whistle. "Now *that* takes some *cojones*."

"Well, if our stories are going to be in print, lads," Kiyoko said, "we better make sure every second of the rest of our time here counts."

"Dead right," Liv said.

Alexa nodded, smiling at her friends. It didn't seem possible that they would all be splitting up again in just two weeks for the holidays, but it made her feel better to know that they'd be back together in the spring. *"Absolutamente,"* she said. "It's all about making our mark, *chiquitas*. Starting this afternoon at Barney's."

"*Aye, aye, aye*, what is taking so long?" Alexa whispered, shifting impatiently from one foot to another as she shoved her gloved hands deeper into her pockets. "*Estoy fria!*"

Kiyoko rolled her eyes. "You look like a penguin doing the meringue. Clearly you're not used to northeast winters, but save the grumbling until after the unveiling, okay? It's not every day we get to see our handiwork on show at the greatest fashion mecca in Midtown."

"And it's all going down in history," Eli said from behind his digicam. He was filming the entire thing for Liv to send to her parents, much to Liv's delight. She gave him one of those isn't-he-just-so-charming looks, and Alexa had to smile, even through her chattering teeth. She was so glad Liv and Eli had made up. They were a great couple, and now that Liv had set things straight with her mother, she seemed to be truly relaxing into the relationship for the first time.

"Come on, Lexa," Mel said. "Don't freeze yet. It's almost time."

They all anxiously listened to Ms. Bishop wrap up her speech from the podium in front of the still-covered Barney's windows. The crowd clapped politely as she thanked the manager of Barney's, once again, for the honor of contributing to the windows.

"Now, I'd like to ask our *Flirt* interns to join me up front," she said. "They all contributed their talent and hours of hard work to create these displays, and they should do the honors of the unveiling."

The girls shared shocked expressions as Emma gave them playful pushes toward the podium.

"*No lo creo,*" Alexa whispered, and even Gen looked genuinely surprised by her aunt's announcement. But, somehow, all six of them made their way up to the windows.

"Ladies and gentlemen," Ms. Bishop said, signaling for the girls to pull the curtains, "we give you 'Naughty and Nice 2007.'"

Alexa let the black curtain billow down around her and smiled as the crowd burst into loud applause. She stepped back and rejoined Liv, Kiyoko, Mel, Gen, and Charlotte to see the full effect.

"*Muy de la banana,*" she said.

"You've got that right, lad," Kiyoko said.

There were Alexa's prints from the "Naughty and Nice" photo shoot in a collage forming the backdrop of each window, mirroring the outfits the mannequins were wearing. Alexa had captured the colors and models with unique angles and lighting, making them look by turns Christmas angels and mischievous elves. Basil Shade's rendition of "Silent Night," complete with Kiyoko's additions, was blaring from the speakers with all of the beautiful noise and bustle of the

Manhattan streets. Gen and Charlotte had created wreaths of beauty products and even some mistletoe with Lancôme Red Fusion lipstick as the berries. Liv's jewelry dangled from the wrists, necks, and ears of the mannequins, and also dripped from the fir trees behind them like dazzling tinsel. A huge replica of a *New York Times* crossword puzzle hung suspended in one of the windows, with quotes from Mel's "Brit Fashion unThamed" feature filling the blanks, and next to it was Maia's painting.

"Mum is going to eat this up," Liv said, grinning at Mel.

"Score one for the granola girl." Mel laughed.

Alexa smiled. The display was *fantastique*—a mish-mash of cosmopolitan chic and eccentricity—just like *Flirt*, and just like the six of them.

As the crowd formed a line to pass by the windows to see everything in more detail, Emma congratulated the girls.

"You've taken the city by storm for the last six months," Emma said. "By the time you finish your internships next spring, *Flirt* will never be the same."

Emma quickly whispered to the girls that she'd see them back at the loft later and disappeared into the crowd, leaving the interns alone with Her Lordship.

Ms. Bishop looked at each of

> **" Score one for the granola girl. "**

the girls in turn, and Alexa couldn't be positive, but she thought she saw a hint of pride in the magazine mogul's eyes. "Now, Jared is waiting to take you all to Club 21 for a celebratory dinner on *Flirt*," Ms. Bishop said, motioning to the *Flirt* corporate driver waiting on 59th Street, "and he'll take you wherever you'd like after that. Emma and I spoke earlier and she agreed to extend your curfew to two A.M., just for tonight, as long as you call to check in at midnight."

"Snap!" Kiyoko said. "I mean, thank you, your high—Ms. Bishop."

Ms. Bishop nodded, then pulled six envelopes from her Prada bag and handed them to the girls. "Just a little holiday bonus, so to speak," she said, the flicker of a smile playing on her lips.

"*¡Qué bueno!*" Alexa cried, peeking inside to see a gift certificate for a full day of service at Bliss Spa inside. She shared thrilled smiles with Mel, Liv, and Kiyoko, and even Gen and Charlotte looked excited.

"I expect to see you all back in the office in January, refreshed and ready to start on the spring issues," Ms. Bishop said, just as Delia stepped to her side with a handful of messages. "And you know better than to disappoint me." With that she swiftly moved away, taking the

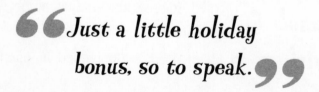

"*Just a little holiday bonus, so to speak.*"

messages from Delia and answering her cell phone all at once. "No, no," they heard her say bitingly into the phone as she walked away. "I said to run the Oscar de la Renta ad at the *front*."

"The 'Bish Who Stole Christmas' is back," Kiyoko said, looking after her. "But," she added, waving her Bliss certificate, "she just proved her heart isn't entirely made of coal."

"Vamanos, chiquitas," Alexa said, throwing her arms around Liv and Mel. "We have the rest of the weekend together. What should we do first after dinner?"

"We could check out Webster Hall," Mel suggested.

"Or Vanquish," Kiyoko said.

"Does it really matter?" Liv asked, laughing.

And suddenly, Alexa realized that it didn't. Not at all. Not as long as they were together.